DR. ORGASM

A VIRGIN AND A BILLIONAIRE ROMANCE

SCARLETT KING
MICHELLE LOVE

HOT AND STEAMY ROMANCE

CONTENTS

Sign Up to Receive Free Books	v
Blurb	vii
1. Chapter 1	1
2. Chapter 2	6
3. Chapter 3	10
4. Chapter 4	15
5. Chapter 5	21
6. Chapter 6	26
7. Chapter 7	35
8. Chapter 8	43
9. Chapter 9	50
10. Chapter 10	57
11. Chapter 11	60
Sign Up to Receive Free Books	65
Preview of Home is Where the Heat Is	67
Prologue	69
Chapter One	77
Chapter Two	85
Chapter Three	95
Other Books By This Author	105
About the Author	107

Made in "The United States" by:

Scarlett King & Michelle Love

© Copyright 2020 – Scarlett King & Michelle Love

ISBN: 978-1-64808-134-7

ALL RIGHTS RESERVED. No part of this publication may be reproduced or transmitted in any form whatsoever, electronic, or mechanical, including photocopying, recording, or by any informational storage or retrieval system without express written, dated and signed permission from the author

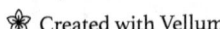 Created with Vellum

SIGN UP TO RECEIVE FREE BOOKS

Sign Up to Receive Free E-Books and Audiobook Codes.

Would you like to read **The Unexpected Nanny, Dirty Little Virgin** and **other romance books** for **free**?

You can sign up to receive these free e-books and audiobooks by typing this link into your browser:

https://www.steamyromance.info/free-books-and-audiobooks-hot-and-steamy/

Or this one:

https://www.steamyromance.info/the-unexpected-nanny-free/

BLURB

Maddy:

It's amazing what you can do when you don't care if you live or die. Like escape from the hellhole where you have been a prisoner for half your life. Or ride off on the back of a hot stranger's motorcycle. Aaron is the first guy I have ever met that I have felt this way about. I like him. I trust him. I want him. But if I follow his lead and start wanting to live again, what happens when someone tries to drag me back into the hell I escaped from?

Aaron:

I'm falling for a mystery girl that I just talked out of jumping off a bridge. I shouldn't let myself. She needs help, support, maybe even protection—not sex. But as I try to show her that life is worth living, nature starts taking its course. Soon enough the best lessons I can teach her are the ones between the sheets ...

and she is more than willing. But I'm about to stumble across an ugly truth about my Maddy that will make me rethink everything—and will put us both in danger.

CHAPTER 1

Aaron

It's almost midnight by the time I drive my motorcycle out of Ravenwood Hospital's sprawling parking lot. It's a foggy night, turning the road into a tunnel and the surrounding forest into something ghostly and surreal. It's the perfect weather for Halloween.

I love Halloween—I've been a horror movie buff since I was ten. I grew up on a ranch twenty miles from town in Wyoming, so the thirty-first of October meant a special dinner, pumpkin lanterns, and a lengthy horror movie marathon instead of trick or treating. I loved those nights.

I'm dead tired and I don't much mind that I won't be home in time for any Halloween parties. Behind my visor, my eyes are bleary from checking and rechecking dozens of forms. It was back-paperwork night in the cardiology wing, and as the youngest director in Ravenwood's hundred-year history, I didn't have any excuse to leave early.

I had two assistants helping me out—Becky, a veteran of the department, and Kate, who is less experienced but a harder worker. I needed both to help me plow through this month's paperwork, which included the annual financial report and an assortment of federal grant applications. Now, each and every last scrap of paper has been filed, recycled, or followed up on, and I'm fleeing back to my mansion before more comes in.

My head stings, my back aches, and I'm dehydrated. I know that enough fluids, a good meal, and a visit to my home gym and jacuzzi will fix everything. Meanwhile, though, I have to get home down a winding coastal road, with wet streets and swirling wind to deal with. Good thing I'm steady under pressure.

At least the rain has let up. The wet branches drip on me as I drive out onto the main road, humming Metallica's "Enter Sandman" under my breath.

Ravenwood sits in the wooded hills just outside Marin County, in one of the most beautiful regions in California. The air is clean here, there's plenty of rain and open land, and the sea goes on forever outside the Golden Gate. The area is at its best in high summer, with warm, slightly misty nights full of stars.

In fall, however, it's ... well, I find it perfect, but some of my coworkers find it creepy as hell. Especially since we have to cross a gorge on our way off hospital grounds, and the spooky looking bridge we have to use is always dark, falling under the shadow of towering trees with no lights to guide the way. At night, you have to use your high beams and pray there are no surprises waiting for you.

I'm trying to sort out what movies to watch as I approach the stretch of road that leads to the bridge. The road is just wide enough that I can see the moon through the break in the trees, sailing ahead of me high and silver, with a pattern that always reminds me of watermarks.

"John Carpenter?" I muse aloud. Classic horror is always

good. Problem is I already did a John Carpenter marathon a few months ago. Though I love his creepy stuff, I need a palate cleanser.

"Huh," I mutter. I have a bad habit of talking to myself when alone.

"*Tales from the Crypt*? Something from the *MST3K* collection?" Nah, too campy. I frown as I go around a turn. I can see the faint shape of the bridge looming half a mile up the road.

"J-horror?" The Japanese have their own very distinct style of horror, and some of the best people in the business these days come from there. I've been working my way through the *Ring* series which, except for the crack-fest of the second movie, has managed to be both poignant and terrifying. I haven't seen the prequel about Sadako, *Ringu o*, and decide to put it on first when I get home.

There's nothing like a Japanese ghost story. Figures in white, with streaming black hair, transformed from demure wives, mothers, and daughters to betrayed, rage-filled entities whose power seems bottomless. The fact that these horrible monsters are often played by fetchingly pretty actresses only adds another layer of creepiness to it all.

I nod to myself, satisfied. That's one movie down to watch while I have my steak and beer. The household staff will be gone for the night except for my security team, but I'm sure I can sort out reheating my dinner.

Too bad I have no date to share movie night with. Being a department head in my mid-thirties tends to eat up all my free time. And a relationship requires a lot more than a quick date or fuck during my few spare hours on weekends.

At least now, with the backlog of paperwork, phone calls, and meetings eliminated, I can think about going out to a bar or something this coming weekend. It's been a while since I even danced with a woman, let alone took one to my bed. I miss it, in that bone-deep way that leads to dirty dreams and the occasional reckless decision.

I'm almost at the bridge. My Harley's headlights splash across the weathered wood and I peer ahead, catching sight of something emerging out of the fog. "What the hell is that?" I mutter.

There is something white standing in a misty patch of moonlight about halfway across the bridge. It's human-sized, if smaller than me—though almost everyone is. It has either black hair or a black shawl hanging over its shoulders, and it's dressed in flowing white—either a robe or a coat.

For a moment, my tired brain goes *oh shit oh shit oh shit* and I'm certain that either this is a nightmare or reality just took a hard left. But a split second later I get hold of myself and let out a laugh as I slow down.

"Oh, man, no way." I'm not looking at a Japanese ghost. I'm looking at a young, living woman who just really looks the part.

I slow down enough to have a better look and to give her a compliment on her costume. Not a catcall. That's not my style. But she did just scare the crap out of me—mission accomplished as far as dressing like Sadako.

As I slow the bike down she squints up at me, holding up one slim, pale hand to shade her eyes. She's not Japanese, though her petite build and straight, silky black hair make me think she could be mixed. Her wide, deep brown eyes catch my attention then, and I find myself falling into them before I can stop myself.

"Uh ..." I manage as I stop and turn the headlight away from her, just enough to keep the glare out of her face. "Hi! Nice costume."

"Costume?" She looks down at herself, and I get a better look at her as I wonder if she's a bit high. She's actually wrapped in a lab coat that is about five sizes too big for her, making it float around her dramatically in the wind. Beneath it, I catch sight of an overlarge pale sweater and the silvery drape of a velvet skirt. It's all too big for her, but she's so waiflike that it almost looks like a deliberate fashion choice. If not, as I thought before, a costume.

"I'm sorry, are you okay?" I ask suddenly. I've seen people with this shocked, sad look on their faces before—usually when I'm talking to the family of someone we lost on the table. It doesn't happen too often, but that haunted expression sticks with you. So I notice it right away.

She stares at me as if she has no idea what to say. The wind picks up, hissing through the pine branches and sending her hair and clothes drifting around her. We watch each other mutely. After a pregnant pause she lifts her head and gives me the saddest smile I have ever seen in my life.

"No," she replies simply, and my heart sinks.

CHAPTER 2

Madelyne

The sky is so enormous, now that I am free. I have been indoors for so long that I feel dizzy as I stare up at the slowly disintegrating clouds, as if I will be overwhelmed if I don't look away. And it's not just the sky; the whole world outside the asylum is vast.

I managed to avoid swallowing some of my meds before bed check, spitting them out and flushing them instead. It's been a good two hours since then—just enough time to slip out and steal clothes from the nurses' lockers and to hike this far down the road. Problem is, the pills still partially dissolved in my mouth before I could get rid of them, so I'm lightheaded as I turn to the man on the motorcycle.

I didn't expect anyone to be out driving this late in the middle of nowhere. The fact that he came from the direction of the hospital makes me a little nervous. But Ravenwood is huge—the campus has three separate complexes on it, including the mental hospital.

It's possible that he doesn't even work in the same building. I try to remind myself of that fact as he dismounts from the bike and pulls off his helmet. When I see his face, everything else leaves my mind for a few moments.

I don't know anything about men or attraction. I haven't had the opportunity to do anything but admire boys from afar. But suddenly my stomach flutters, I feel a warm flush in my cheeks, and the dark thoughts that have been swirling through my head part like clouds before the moon.

His hair is a sort of tawny brown color, like a lion's mane—shot with gold threads that reflect the glow from the motorcycle headlights in sparks. It stands up from a high forehead, mussed by his helmet. The lean, tanned face beneath is prickled with blond stubble along his jawline. His mouth is generous and well-shaped, and his narrow green eyes stare into mine like he's looking right through me.

He's also huge, I realize as he dismounts his motorcycle and stands up straight. He looms over me, and only his gentle expression keeps me from freaking out and putting more space between us.

"What's your name?" he asks me softly.

I blink at him, reluctant to tell him. He could hear, later, about a missing patient named Madelyne at this very hospital. But then I just shake my head slightly, amused with myself. Unless he's a regular visitor to the hospital, he's not likely to hear anything. I doubt they'd let my name get out to the public. "Madelyne."

"That's a pretty name. I'm Aaron. Do you need some kind of help?" He tilts his head slightly, and I shrink a little under his piercing gaze. He's intimidating without even meaning to be, even when he's being kind.

"I ... no. There's ... not much that can be done, really. I'm just going to ... spend a little time around here, that's all." I struggle to sound casual and wonder why it's so hard for me to keep the shaking out of my voice suddenly. "You can ... you can go on. I'll be okay. Really."

The gorge is deep and shadowy, with rocks like jutting fangs. I can hear rushing water down there. The whole idea of throwing myself over the railing terrifies me.

But if there's one thing I know, it's that they will catch me if I stay on the run. I have no family, no friends, no money, nowhere to go. It doesn't matter that I don't have any of the illnesses that I was hospitalized for, except, of course, for the depression. The doctor will not let me be free as long as I am alive.

Aaron gives a deep, resigned sigh, and before I know what he's doing he leans against the weathered railing, not so inconspicuously placing himself between me and the brink. He folds his powerful arms and the leather of his jacket creaks against his biceps.

"I don't think you're going to be okay if I leave you, sweetheart," he says in a calm tone that leaves me with tears brimming in my eyes. "As a matter of fact, I think that if I leave you here, they'll be pulling you out of the gorge tomorrow morning."

"Oh, that's nonsense. I—" I start, then realize that I have started fidgeting. "I'm ... I just ..."

"Look," Aaron says softly, catching my eye. "I don't know what's brought you out here like this. I don't know what you're going through, and I'm not gonna judge. But I am gonna ask you something."

I stop fidgeting and lick my lips, gathering my wits. How did he know what I was planning? I wipe my eyes impatiently. "What?"

"If you don't care whether you live or die anyway, then how about you come take a ride with me instead?" His smile is charming, his tone reasonable. But his eyes bore into mine, seeking my answer.

This wasn't in my plan. Confusion swamps me again and I

stand still, blinking back at him. "Why would you do that?" I ask.

He shrugs. "I can't just leave you. But I can't tell you what to do with your life either. If you don't mind my saying so, you look a little ambivalent about the whole ... situation here. I figure maybe a nice ride will help you clear your head."

I hesitate. It's true that I have nothing left to lose. It's true that if anything, taking this man up on his offer gives me a chance at a running start before the doctor finds out I'm missing.

Escaping with my life might be possible after all. Or if it isn't, maybe I can just have a little fun before I go back to my first option.

I walk over to the motorcycle, which gleams black and silver in the moonlight. It's huge and powerful-looking, like its owner. Maybe he's a biker that was discharged from the emergency wing. Maybe he's not the type to turn me in.

Nothing to lose but my life, and I was an inch from giving that up anyway.

I look back at him and nod. "Let's go."

CHAPTER 3

Aaron

"I've never ridden a motorcycle," she confesses, and I smile and pull my spare helmet from my saddlebag.

I'm so relieved that she agreed to my plan to keep her from killing herself that it feels like a weight has lifted off my chest. I came up with it by the seat of my pants.

But I became a doctor for a reason: to save lives. I wasn't about to just leave her there.

"Here. I'll get on, and you climb on after me. I'll show you where to put your feet." I look her over. "Do you have anything to put your hair up with?"

She didn't, so I take a strip of gauze from my saddlebag's emergency kit and tie her hair in a low ponytail. "Here you go."

Mom and Dad have never understood why I would leave their land in Wyoming, which expands every year and is full of every possible luxury or bit of wilderness that a man could possibly need. But I wanted to make my own mark. It wasn't enough for me to simply inherit Father's pharmaceutical company—or the ranch built by its wealth—and coast on his achievements.

So med school it was. And then my specialty, and then my residency. I started climbing the ladder at Ravenwood in my late twenties, when most people my age were still finishing grad school. I was far too focused on my goal to let myself waste time.

My attention is brought back to Madelyn as she adjusts her ponytail. She's skittish, shifting nervously when I touch her. I don't feel too bad about that. I don't know what hell she has been through, but as long as she isn't jumping off a fucking bridge I figure she's better off for my intervention. I just know I can't expect her to treat me like a hero because of it.

I help her get the helmet on, wrap her in my leather jacket, and get on the bike. After a few moments of hesitation, she gets on behind me. I feel her arms slip around my chest under my arms, and feel an unexpected jolt of pleasure.

Shit. This woman is distraught enough to be contemplating suicide. I can't even think about my attraction to her until she's stable. I absolutely have to make certain that she's okay first.

First, do no harm, I think as I rev the engine. "Okay. Hold onto me firmly, and if you get scared, let me know."

She buries the front of her helmet in my back as we take off down the road. Her arms squeeze me tight—she's already scared. But she doesn't stiffen up and she doesn't tell me to stop, so I keep going.

There's a possibility that she's playing me and will jump off the damn bike as soon as we get up to speed. I don't know what I'll do if she does that, besides get an ambulance here as fast as I can.

In a way, we're both forced to have faith in each other. As we leave the bridge behind and drive off into the dark, I can feel her relax just a little, and continue to do so bit by bit as we get closer to the coastal highway. We can't talk, and besides monitoring her and the road, I'm pretty much left to my thoughts.

I was made head of Ravenwood Hospital's Cardiology Department early last year after the old head, Dr. Emil Blanchley, retired abruptly after breaking the nose of the head of the psychiatric wing. I can't say that I blame him one bit for landing that punch—Dr. Westridge is a prick. But rules are rules, and while some members of the board chuckled about it, Blanchley was told to retire immediately if he wished to keep his pension.

I've been scrambling to clean up after him ever since, going through years of neglected paperwork that has demanded many late nights. Blanchley might've been an incredible doctor, but a pencil pusher he was not. I've been forced to plow through it in chunks while struggling to keep up on current papers. All this administrative crap frustrates me most because it does nothing to directly serve patients.

I know it's pretty unusual for a department head to have a hero complex, but I *have* helped save lives since taking the position. It's just been indirect, not hands-on. But I do everything that I possibly can.

Everything from getting a kid from a poor family a transplant to keeping the department on the cutting edge of modern cardiology medicine; I go after it all with everything I have. I'm not an ex-army tough guy like my Dad, but I still fight—for my patients and for my department. Even if I have to fund the battles with my own money.

This mess with Madelyne is just another day at the office in that respect. I'm trying to save a life. But the question is, how best to do so?

If she's suicidal, by law, I'm supposed to turn around and hand her right over to the psychiatric wing for a 48-hour hold. If I don't and she kills herself, I'm liable. But if I do ... she'll end up in the hands of the worst department head on the entire Ravenwood staff.

Dr. Westridge isn't just a bad doctor, he's a bad administrator. All kinds of rumors fly around this place about the psychiatric wing. Unacceptably high suicide levels. Unexplained deaths. Complaints of abuse.

He and I have clashed on a variety of subjects, including his insistence on keeping certain mentally ill cardiac patients in restraints, even when it endangers them. He loves drugs, often keeping his patients on levels of sedatives that sometimes endanger them as well. And he loves petty power plays— even among his equals—making him nearly impossible to work with.

The rest of us on staff keep hearing reports of complaints and lawsuits filed against Westridge and wonder when he will finally run out of money for settlements. As far as I am concerned, he doesn't belong anywhere near a patient—ever. But so far luck, money, and a talented lawyer have protected him from any serious consequences.

I can't send Madelyne to him. I know too well what will happen if I do. The man will make everything worse. He seems to have a talent for it.

If I take her across state lines, though, and into a major city like Portland, I can get her into a hospital with someone who has to be more competent and ethical than Westridge. Now that she's starting to calm down, maybe I can get her to agree to that as a plan if she needs to be hospitalized.

We emerge from the access road onto the coastal highway and sweep northward along its cliff-hugging curves, the sea shimmering under the moon to one side of us. I can see the gleam of lights from little hamlets dotting the hills above us, and the sheets of cloud from the dying storm have all lowered into a hilltop crown of fog.

It's a view worth living to see. I hope my passenger notices.

I check in with her, reaching back carefully to pat her hand with my gloved one. She squeezes my fingers briefly and I go back to driving, temporarily satisfied. *Well, she didn't bail back on the road, and I doubt she's going to jump now that we're out here.*

On we drive, past several cliffside houses and a rest stop, until finally I slow down to take a break at a turn-off that leads up the hill to my home. It has a couple of benches and an old phone booth. I pull up by one of the benches and get off to stretch my legs and talk to her.

"How was that?" I ask as she awkwardly pulls off her helmet.

"It was ... a little overwhelming, but I ... I'm glad you took me for a ride. Where are we going?" Her voice sounds so hesitant and tentative that I wonder if she thinks I'm leaving her here.

I open my mouth to offer her a ride back to my place, and then I have to stop and wonder at my motives. *Behave.* "Well," I say slowly, "where do you want to go?"

She looks out over the ocean silently, wrapping her arms around herself. "As far from here as we can," she finally murmurs. "That's where I want to go."

I think about the two days off work I have coming, and mentally count the cash left in my wallet. I live more modestly than I have to, so I usually have a decent amount of liquid assets. I might have to visit a bank at some point, but ...

"Any specifics?" But of course, she shakes her head. She really wasn't thinking past tonight. I'm glad I was smart enough to pick up on that.

"All right, up the coastline it is, then. I'll just get us some clothes to change into in the nearest large town." I give her a smile, and see a gleam of something like hope in her eyes.

CHAPTER 4

Madelyne

I freeze up when he asks me where I want to go. Up until half an hour ago, I didn't want to be anywhere. But now, staring out over the silver sea and the wild night stretching above it, I start to think once again about an escape that doesn't involve dying.

If I can get across state lines, I can ditch this hot but potentially overcurious guy and take off. By the time that Aaron gets back home and discovers that the police are searching for me, I'll be nothing but a memory to him. I don't know much about the outside world after ten years locked away in the hospital, but I'm certain I can figure out some way to survive.

At least I'll finally be free, even if I don't last long.

Half an hour after I tell him "north," we make our first stop. It's a little too close to the hospital for comfort, and the lights are too bright for me. But it's a public place, it's dry and warm, and best of all, nobody here is paying attention to much of anything besides their meals.

We're sitting in a chrome, white, and red fifties-style café that's half full of tourists and truckers. It's done up for Halloween, with clusters of carved pumpkins and those jointed cardboard monsters that they always put up in the nursing station back at the hospital. Over half the people there, including a sleepy gaggle of kids, are in costume, making my weird "borrowed" outfit look normal.

Good. I absolutely cannot afford to stand out in any way.

Aaron is in no rush, and I can't afford to let on that I am. *Just act normal,* I tell myself firmly as I ball up in a chair and glance nervously around.

"I just really need coffee if we're going for a long ride, and this is the best local place." He gives me that smile again. It's like a flash of light cutting through the gray clouds around me, and I can't help but try on a small smile in return. It feels strange on my face.

"I understand." I take a sip of my own. It's bitter, and I wince and dump sugar and cream into the mug as I realize that I've never actually had coffee before.

He smiles a little. "They make the coffee strong here. Sorry, I should have warned you."

"That's okay, I just ..." I have to stifle a cough. *Yikes. Do they use this stuff to clean floors?*

He presses his lips together and looks away like he's trying not to laugh. "I've gotten so used to it that I don't notice. Hospital staff go through strong coffee like water."

I feel my blood turn cold for a moment before forcing my smile to stay on. *Crap. I knew he might work at the hospital. He's not from the psych staff ... who is he?* "Oh, you work at Ravenwood?"

"Yeah, I'm the head of the cardiology department." He flashes a boyish grin that says the opposite of "respected senior hospital staff" and I just stare at him. "We went through paperwork hell today, so I was working late. Pretty glad of it now."

"Yeah," I reply, a little breathlessly. He's talking calmly, openly. Not patronizingly or demandingly, or in broken bits of sentences or stream of consciousness. Not like a doctor or attendant, not like a patient either. Like a man—an ordinary man.

It is such a new experience for me after so many years seeing only the same few people day after day that it refreshes and fascinates me. Everything about him fascinates me, especially his clear, honest concern for a total stranger. Suddenly, even if I still don't care if I live or die any more, I realize that I'm curious about some part of life again. "I'm ... glad that you did too."

The look of relief on his face surprises me. Why does he care so much about what happens to me? Nobody else ever has. The gesture is so alien, in fact, that something in me starts whispering about how he must have some ulterior motive.

Maybe he wants sex. If that's true, he's going a long way to get it. I have mixed feelings about the idea. On the one hand, I know nothing about sex and know I can't handle being hurt again so soon. On the other, he's both hot and kind—a combination that I have never seen before.

I really hope it isn't all an act.

"I'm pretty glad to hear you say that. Truth is, I was worried when you were pretty obviously thinking of jumping into the damn gorge." He takes a bite of his muffin while I blink at him, at a loss for what to say. He chews, swallows, and goes on, never breaking eye contact. "You want to tell me why?"

My stomach does a flip. I can't tell him about escaping the hospital if he works there, or he'll be obliged to bring me back. So I decide to piece together the bits of truth that I can tell him. I'm careful not to lie—he deserves better than that, and he's smart enough that he would probably be able to tell.

"Well, I ... have been on my own since the age of ten, and I ended up in the custody of someone really ... terrible." I swallow more coffee and let it warm me. The cream has helped that bitter taste, but it still reminds me of soap.

"And ...?" his eyes narrow slightly, and I freeze for a moment, wondering if I'm being foolish by giving him any truth at all. But what's my best option? I can't just tell him nothing, not any more than I can lie to him.

"He had control over me. I mean, I was technically a ward of the state, but, um ... he was the one with custody. And it was ... nasty. And I'd rather not get into the details." I manage a bite of my blueberry muffin. It's fruity and subtler than I'm used to; everything at the hospital was blandly sweet, and I barely ever tasted so much as an apple.

He looks troubled but nods. "That's understandable. So what happened? Did you become depressed?"

"No," I say sadly. "I finally escaped from him. But ... I was with him for ten years. Since I was a kid. No schooling, no socializing, no access to the outside world."

I spread my hands, wishing I was a lot more eloquent. Maybe if I had more practice at normal conversation I would be better at this.

He's staring at me in horror. "So ..." he says finally in a low, shocked tone, "you were someone's ... captive?"

"He always said it was for my own good. That I was too sick to go outside. But the truth is ... it was a game to him. A power trip."

My head is already clearing. This is the longest I have gone without a full dose of tranquilizers in ten years.

"He sounds insane," he mumbles in amazement, setting down his cup.

"Yes, he is all of that and more," I agree distractedly. "He doesn't legally have the right to keep me anywhere anymore, since I'm twenty now. I should have been able to get away when I turned eighteen, but he simply ... didn't let me go."

It was worse than that—a lot worse. The drugs, the mind games—the doctor constantly trying to tell me that I was sicker than I was, and that I could not trust my own mind. It makes me sick to think about, and I quickly distract myself with nibbling on my muffin.

"How did you escape?" He takes a swallow of his coffee, still staring at me wide-eyed.

"I managed to keep from swallowing some of my tranquilizers and slipped out. I've never given th—him any trouble, so I was never watched too closely after lights out." It's all true, and comes out smoothly. Let him think I'm talking about a private home and not a ward in his own hospital.

"Jesus. Do you know what this guy had you on, and where he was getting it?" He sounds outraged—for me. That's something completely new.

I stare at him, really not sure what to say. I, of course, know the meds that have been forced on me: three amber ovals of Seroquel totaling maybe 1200 milligrams daily, and four two-milligram bars of Xanax totaling eight milligrams. They were given to me at precise times, day and night, so that I was always being interrupted to swallow more pills. I couldn't even sleep through the night.

"I don't actually know. He didn't put me on them because I'm depressed; they were all tranquilizers." That's as specific as I'll get, I decide. If I show too much knowledge of my meds he'll likely start asking questions about who explained them to me. It wasn't that control freak, after all—it was one of the nurses. I'll plead ignorance and hope it doesn't matter all that much.

"This guy sounds crazy. I wonder if he was supposed to be taking them himself and just pushed them off onto you." He drains his mug and gestures to the waitress, a chubby redhead wandering around in a pair of black cat ears. "Do you think he'll come after you?"

"I'm absolutely sure of it. He's ... possessive. He will want to get me back. And I would rather die than go back."

It's the truth, and it's all the truth I can manage.

"So you're not suicidally depressed—" he starts, and I cut him off more sharply than I intend.

"No. He always told me I was crazy so I wouldn't have any confidence in myself, but it's crap. I'm depressed because of my circumstances, and I wanted to kill myself because I thought it was the only way out. You came by and offered me an alternative. I took it." I stare him firmly in the eyes, clinging tight to my one scrap of pride.

He rakes a hand back through his spiky bronze hair and sighs. "That's both a relief and a problem, because if even half of what you are saying is true, then you have bigger issues than just recovering from depression."

"I know," I reply softly, picking at my muffin, then look up at him again. "That's why I need you to get me as far away from here as possible. If you really want to help me, that is what I need."

Those intense green eyes hold me captive. I have no idea what he thinks of me right now. I only pray that he believes me, and sympathizes.

Then, slowly, he nods. "Well, for what it's worth, I believe you. I'll make arrangements for some accommodations in southern Oregon. That way we'll have a place to shoot for by the time we both wear out."

I manage another tiny smile. Something like hope is creeping into my heart, and I nod. "That sounds fine. I know I won't be able to sleep for a long time as is."

CHAPTER 5

Aaron

The story that Madelyne tells me is horrifying. I have no doubt that it's true, or at least mostly true. Her state of mind, the daze she's been slowly coming out of since I met her, her oversized clothes—probably stolen from someone in the man's household, or a neighbor—they all help verify her story. But there's one more thing I can check to confirm things for me.

"Can I see your wrist?" I ask very, very gently. She blinks at me before slowly extending it across the table. I push back the loose sleeves covering her forearm, and a shudder goes through me.

Soft restraints only leave a mark if they are tied too tightly or left on too long. Madelyne has a faint, shiny scar around her wrist, along with fresh irritation. Someone basically had her chained up ... for a long time, by looks of it.

Shuddering, I nod and let her go. "Okay," I murmur, my mind racing.

She's telling the truth. She's pale because she's been indoors. She's squinting against the light. She's underweight, and she is only starting to come out of being listless. This girl was a captive somewhere.

The very thought makes me want to find whatever guy did this and beat the living hell out of him. It's a deep, primal urge—to protect her and avenge us both against a nameless prick who has left me cleaning up his mess.

I can't moderate my reaction very well around her. It's just too intense. The hell that she has been through shocks and infuriates me.

I'm a doctor. Saving lives is my business. But if I ever find the man who did this to her on my table, my Hippocratic Oath will be severely tested.

Maybe she doesn't tell me the rest because it's even more horrible. Maybe I don't need to know any more of the specifics. She can lay them out to the cops when she feels strong enough.

Right now, I just have to get her safe and get her well enough that she can go her way without my having to worry about her. I don't imagine it will take that much time, and if I need to, I will take some time off. I'm not sure I can focus on anything else now that I know this woman is literally running from a criminal who stole her life away.

It really doesn't help that I'm attracted to her. And I really, really am. It's not just that dark-haired, pale-skinned waif look that I like so much. It's not just the way I keep falling into those big, velvety eyes of hers. It's ... deeper than that.

Relationships forged in crisis rarely get anywhere, I remind myself and focus on finishing another cup of coffee. "You doing all right on the bike so far?"

"It's better now that I'm not so dizzy. The pills are starting to wear off, which is good." Her lips twist. "The drugs were as much to imprison me as the restraints and the locked doors."

"But you have no idea what he put you on." I frown, knowing

that a lot of tranquilizers have withdrawal symptoms. Ugly ones. "Can you tell me the shape and color of the pills?"

"One was oval and kind of cream colored. The other was kind of shaped like a chocolate bar, but small. He never let me examine them." Her gaze drifts away from me for a moment and I can tell she's hiding something. But at least what she has told me is a start.

I nod, pulling out my smart phone for my app version of the *Desk Reference*. "Rectangular white pills with multiple division lines?" She nods. *Oops, that's Xanax bars. That's what they do with the higher dose pills so they can be broken up into smaller doses easier.*

I brace myself to give her some bad news. "Okay. That adds a little wrinkle. If one of the things you were on is a high dose of Xanax, you absolutely have to have some on hand in order to step down. Otherwise, you are going to not only get a lot worse mentally, you're going to get really sick."

I am not kidding, and I make sure she knows that by keeping my eye contact focused and my tone deadly serious. "There's a withdrawal syndrome associated with that class of drugs, so you can't just go cold turkey. Fortunately, I'm an MD and can write you a prescription."

"That's going considerably out of your way," she protests. I hear the wariness behind her voice and I can't blame her for that either.

"It's all right. I have two days off and can take more time if I need to. I'm assuming that you don't feel comfortable going to the police quite yet?" My guess is she isn't there yet. She barely even trusts me right now, and if she's been trapped for ten years she may not know who else she can trust.

She shakes her head. "I have to figure out what I'm going to say to them. Right now, my kidnapper's one of those pillar of the community types. Lots of money, lots of people working for him, and I don't ... I don't know how far his reach is. He may trick the police into turning me back over to him."

A tiny alarm bell goes off in my head as she tells me this. I start to wonder whether her judgment of things is trustworthy. She might be telling the truth, or she might just be sincerely describing her delusions.

I like her. I want to help her. And though I am pushing the feeling down as deep as I can, I want her. So I decide to slowly gather enough information on her as I work on winning her trust, then I can run a search and see what the Internet has to say.

"I wish I could just stop taking those stupid drugs," she sighs in frustration. "But I can't afford to get sick either." Her chin trembles suddenly, and she looks down. "I—I thought I was done with walking around in a haze all day."

"You will be soon enough," I reassure her. "I just wish I knew what your actual diagnosis is."

"Major depressive disorder," she mutters, looking embarrassed. "Starting at about age nine. No accompanying anxiety. He didn't put me on tranquilizers because I needed them. He needed me ... compliant."

God, how I hate that word right now. The despair that enters her eyes as she delves into those memories is hard to witness. "Okay. I just want to make sure you won't have some kind of crisis because you're stepping down off your meds."

"If what you're hinting at is true," she mused, "the real crisis would be the withdrawal."

"Now that's very true," I admit. "Not just the psychological symptoms but the physical ones. I'm sure you like to do things like sleeping and keeping down food."

She winces, and hurriedly takes a big bite of her muffin. "Yes, I like them very much."

I rub my temple, doing my best to keep my hopes up that

this will get resolved without a big mess. But meanwhile, I'm thinking about the room I'll be renting us as a destination, and what might happen when we get there. I keep *trying* not to think about it, but it's always there in the back of my head now.

It's taking advantage if I touch her. Isn't it? I'm not even sure anymore.

Don't make the first move, I warn myself, and prepare to plow through a disappointing night if she doesn't have any interest. I just wish that I didn't keep catching myself wondering what will happen if she does.

CHAPTER 6

Madelyne

We spend hours on the road, just flying along through the darkness with the moon and stars above and the sea shining out to one side. Now and again we pass a house clinging to the hillside that is decorated for Halloween in colored lights and jack-o-lanterns. I watch it all in wonder from my perch on the back of the Harley.

Eventually we turn inland and head north toward the state line. The trees get bigger, the terrain more mountainous, and the air even cleaner. Now and again a few cars or a big truck pass us, but not often.

It's been so long since I rode or drove anywhere. I'm too exhilarated to be scared. After all, if I have nothing to lose, why fear my possible death?

I don't feel any withdrawal from the doctor's chemical shackles yet. If anything, I feel better and better the further we get from the hospital. I can start to pay attention to things besides fear, despair, and isolation—good things, hopeful things.

Like touching someone, and being touched. That's new, at least in any pleasant context. My arms stay around Aaron as he sends us roaring down the highway, and I have to admit ... it's pretty comfortable.

He's so big and warm. He's kind, he's thoughtful, and he saved my life. I have already confided in him more than I have in anyone for years, and he's helping me more than I ever expected anyone would.

I want to be close to him. I can't get enough of looking at him, of touching him, of smelling his scent. As the drugs finish wearing off, I can feel what he does to me, and it's so natural and painless that I can't resist it.

Something ... normal. Something other women pursue. Love, sex ... a relationship, or even just a one-night stand.

Though I've spent half my life in drug-fueled captivity, I'm not entirely ignorant to the realities of the outside world. Sometimes a sympathetic nurse would let me watch TV shows when the doctor was away, giving me glimpses of what my life could be like if I ever escaped. When I wasn't so lucky, I passed my time by eavesdropping on all the nurses and doctors of the ward —they loved to gossip about their love lives, and those of their co-workers, whenever they'd get the chance.

Though I might have seen and heard a few things about the real world, all of that is unknown territory for me, just like pretty much everything else adults do. Driving a car, holding down a job, paying rent on an apartment—none of it is in any way familiar to my life. But they are all practical things and are pursued because you have to do them if you want to survive.

Love—of any kind—isn't necessary. I have survived without it for most of my life. Doing so hurt, but I managed. As for sex ... I barely thought about it with all those drugs in my system.

Now, clinging to Aaron's back while we roar on through the dark, I wonder again if he's expecting sex from me when we get to this bed and breakfast he's arranged for us in Medford. It will be tough telling him just how totally inexperienced I am at such things if that's the case. Based off what I've told him so far, he probably already suspects my ignorance.

Maybe it won't come up. Maybe I'm reading this wrong. Maybe he's not interested in a traumatized virgin. Or maybe he won't care.

It's so beautiful out here, taking the long, winding road through the trees. I like the company too, even though we can't talk with our helmets on. Maybe that last part is good—after all, I really don't have much practice at conversation, and I'm worried I'll end up messing up.

I'm worried I'll end up messing sex up too. But ... maybe he'll be understanding. From what little I know about men, they'll put up with a lot if it means they'll get laid.

Then again, who am I trying to fool, really? What do I know about men's desires? I barely know anything about my own, except for the fact that being close to Aaron feels really nice.

Maybe I'm overthinking things. Just being around him has me confused, even more than the disorientation of finally being out of my cage. If I end up sleeping with him, I'll be happy as long as it's not too terrible. It's yet another thing I didn't ever expect I would get to experience.

Just over the state line, we pull over at a rest stop—this one's big, with a public toilet and several big trucks parked in the lot. I need the break worse than I want to admit, and can only get off the motorcycle with his help. "How are you doing?" he asks me again as I pull my helmet off.

I do a quick once-over. I'm more clearheaded than ever, though I do feel tense, and I feel like I'm just not going to be able to sleep anytime soon. My muscles are stiff from clinging to the bike, and I have the beginnings of a headache. "Sore, but not too bad. I just need to walk around."

"Good." He looks over at the small truck stop store. "Bathrooms are around back if you need them. You want something to drink?"

Anything but coffee. I try and remember what I used to like before everything I drank turned into institutional apple juice. "Chocolate milk," I declare after a moment.

"Chocolate milk?" he laughs a little. "That's a kid's drink."

I feel my words catch in my throat. My eyes narrow and I actually get a little angry. The tranquilizers must really be wearing off. "Yeah, and the last time I could pick my own drinks I was *ten*. So don't tease."

He backs off immediately. "Of course not. Sorry about that." And he gives me that charming, sweet smile again, and my anger evaporates. "Chocolate milk it is."

There aren't very many people around, just one guy gassing up his truck, a few trucks with a light shining or music playing from their cabs as truckers bunk for the night, and us. It makes me a little nervous—but I go around to the back of the building to take advantage of the smallish, dingy women's room.

I'm finishing up in one of the three steel stalls when I hear the outside door open and a heavy tread come in. I figure that one of the truckers is female and don't pay much attention as I fix my clothes. The footsteps stop, and I don't hear anything further, but I'm barely even thinking about it as I open the door and step out.

There's a gigantic, scruffy blond man in dirty jeans and a red baseball cap standing in the middle of the women's restroom, grinning gap-toothed at me while my brain skips a beat. "Well, hello there, little lady," he drawls, his calloused mitts flexing as he takes a step toward me. "We're gonna have some fun."

I don't know where the scream comes from. I screamed a lot for the first year I was at the hospital, back when I was ten and still furious that my mother had thrown me into that hellhole.

But after that, I got ... disciplined ... enough whenever I raised my voice that I stopped.

For the last few years, I've gone silent when I'm afraid, thanks to almost a decade of conditioning. But this time I let out a shriek that startles my would-be rapist into freezing briefly. With no way to get out around him, I dart back into the stall, slamming the door and leaning on it with all my strength.

Please let Aaron have heard me, please let him come look please please ...

The prick lets out an outraged yell and bulls forward, smashing into the stall door with such force that my teeth rattle together. "You stupid fuckin' whore! You come out here right now!"

My brain feels like it's about to shut off from terror. He slams into the door again—but between the sturdy metal and my leaning on the other side, he can't force it open. That doesn't stop him from trying though, slamming into it until the metal groans and my back feels like he's kicking me right in the spine.

Then, to my horror, he crouches and tries to grab my ankles. His big hands claw at my skirt and past it, and I skitter backwards.

I'm screaming again, so hard my throat feels like it's going to burst. He's got his head and one shoulder in under the door while I stand on the toilet, and he's reaching for me again when suddenly a familiar deep voice shouts, "Hey!"

The man freezes, a flash of fear dissolving the lewd glee on his face, and he yanks himself out of the stall to confront Aaron.

"The fuck do you think you're doing to my girl, you hillbilly piece of shit?" Aaron demands as he stomps up.

I see the man straighten, and watch in horror through the crack around the edge of the door as he pulls out a large knife. "I don't see how that's any of your business, boy." He spits on the floor and waves his weapon slightly. "Besides, I figure that cooze ain't yours if you can't keep her."

Strangely, Aaron's response to this is to smile. "Are you absolutely sure you want to do this?"

"Leave me to my business with this slut before I cut you," the man snarls, lunging.

I don't exactly see what Aaron does in response thanks to my narrow field of vision. I just hear a hard thud and see the man skid suddenly backward, wincing and holding his arm while the knife clatters to the concrete floor. "Fuck—!" he chokes out, sounding astonished.

Aaron's shoe comes down on the knife and he kicks it behind him as the prick lunges at him again. I watch as Aaron backfists the man almost casually and bounces him off the back wall. "What was that?" he snaps. "You're terribly sorry about the misunderstanding, and you're going to run away now before I break your fucking neck?"

"Fuck you—"

Another backfist. The man spits a tooth and slumps down the wall, his eyes enormous, as if he can't fully comprehend what is happening to him.

Aaron turns to my stall. "You all right in there, sweetheart?" he asks me very gently.

"I'm okay!" My voice breaks and trembles, but I'm telling the truth. "He just gave me a scare." I undo the bent latch with some difficulty, then hurry out and dart for the door.

Aaron stays between me and the slumped over creep as we walk out. He takes the knife with him, like a trophy. I don't question it—I'm too grateful and relieved.

Relieved ... and tingling all over. I should be absolutely terrified, but instead, I keep thinking of him beating that creep to a pulp and feel surges of excitement that I just can't understand.

He defended me. He didn't just talk about it, he did it. And that guy that I was so scared of folded in seconds.

He saved my life again. Who is this doctor? How did he manage to walk into my life at just the right time?

He ushers me back over to the motorcycle and turns to me. "Do we call the police?"

It's a terrible idea. I can tell he doesn't fully believe me when I talk about how the doctor is a master manipulator who could easily get the police on his side. I want that creep back there to get locked up so he can't do this again, but …

"Let's call anonymously and then leave. I don't want to get caught up here." I feel cold now. I shiver and pull his leather jacket closer around me.

He watches me a moment longer, then nods slowly. "I understand. Fine." He pulls out his cellphone.

I watch the back corner of the building as he makes the call, wary of the trucker emerging from the bathroom and heading for us again. But he doesn't come out our side, and he doesn't come around the other side and walk out toward the trucks.

The longer we stand there waiting with Aaron on hold with 911 and me shivering and watching, the worse I start to feel. I can feel my adrenaline leaving and my mood crashing, the depression flaring up now that I'm emotionally exhausted.

I know Aaron's with me now and I'm safe, but it was far too close a call. Just a few more seconds and that man would have dragged me out of the stall by the legs. The ugly side of the world is taking the shine off my newfound freedom, and my heart aches.

Finally, he hangs up and glances in the direction I have been watching steadily. "Did he ever come out? I know I didn't hit him hard enough to knock him out."

"I d-don't think so." Without expecting or wanting to, I let out a low, gulping sob.

Embarrassed, I cover my face with my hands. The cold inside me grows so intense that I shudder violently—and then the dam breaks and I'm weeping openly for the first time in years.

My emotions come to a boil as every ugly thing I've been pushing out of my head comes crashing back in. I feel a surge of fear, knowing I'm not supposed to be showing this much emotion.

It's the conditioning. The doctor wanted me calm. Compliant. Doll-like, as he had tried with several of the other young women in his care. Even though I know it's from the years of brainwashing the doctor forced on me, I can't help but feel anxious and ashamed of my emotions on top of everything.

Shit. I sob into my hands, and hate myself for not being able to stop it.

I don't realize that Aaron's talking to me at first, and even then I can only hear the warm, comforting tones of his voice, not the words. My heart is banging away in my ears as I cry uncontrollably.

But then suddenly, I'm enfolded in warmth.

My eyes fly open as my cheek hits his collarbone and I feel his arms tighten around me. He's murmuring soothing things in my ear, petting my hair, telling me that it will be all right. I can feel his steady heartbeat against my breasts and the heat of his body rolling off of him and soaking into my chilled bones.

I sob and wrap my arms around him, hiding my face in his chest. I listen to his steady heartbeat and low murmurs, and faster than I ever would have expected, I feel the thoughts and memories stop torturing me and ebb away. And even then, I do not let him go.

It feels so good to be held and comforted, and I realize as my skin starts to tingle that I've been starved for touch. The right kind of touch, from the right person.

Then something strange happens. His heartbeat starts picking up, and I feel a shiver go through him. His breath catches.

His muscles flex as he pulls me a fraction closer, and I feel how much of his strength he's holding back from me and lose my breath. He could hurt me terribly ... but he never would, would he? His strength, used like this, just makes me feel safer.

Neither one of us wants to pull away. I can feel it. And then I feel something else that confirms it, and sends a hot blush across my cheeks.

The firm lump pressing against my stomach is unfamiliar to me. I've never been this close to any man outside of the doctor and one of his attendants. Sex, lucky for me, was never on either of their agendas. Here, though ... the discovery that I turn Aaron on makes me smile instead of shudder.

Whether it was his intent at the beginning or not, he's interested. What a strange thing! What an exciting, new thing—to be desired by someone that I want as well!

The faint sound of sirens in the distance shocks us out of our embrace. He lets me go, glancing around, as do I. If the man has left the bathroom, he didn't return to the parking lot. It's possible that he ran off into the woods, but I can't afford to stick around and point that out to the police.

"We should make ourselves scarce now," Aaron says in a husky voice, and I nod, stepping away from him. We put on our helmets and climb on the bike, and I feel him shiver pleasantly when I wrap my arms around him. By the time the police get near the rest stop, we are already roaring off down the road.

CHAPTER 7

Aaron

I'm a little worried that I may have accidentally killed that fat fuck who went after Madelyne. I wasn't entirely in control when I hit him. Not after hearing her screams and seeing him crawling under the stall door like an animal trying to get at her.

HALF of me wanted to check before we leave, but that would've been too risky. Not just because of the police, of whom Madelyne seems strangely skittish, but because if I had laid eyes on that would-be rapist again I might have finished the damn job and beaten him to death.

HOLDING Madelyne in my arms after that adrenaline-fueled mess had a predictable result. Her slim body pressed against mine, clinging to me, set off one hell of a boner. And it won't go away for a long time.

I DRIVE for most of the next hour at half-staff, just from her arms around me.

More clouds are starting to roll in by the time we get to the bed and breakfast. I promised a fat bonus to the owner to cover the inconvenience of getting up to check us in. Good as my word, I count out ten twenties for the sour-faced old man behind the counter as he stares coldly at us with watery hazel eyes, lips twitching with some unvoiced disapproval.

I TAKE the key and swipe my card, and we head upstairs to the room. It turns out to be quaint, pretty, and a bit cramped, with a big four-poster bed, two narrow closets, and a window that overlooks a large forest-backed pond. Madelyne trails in after me, her body language gone tight and nervous again.

I LOCK the door and turn to her. "Hey. What is it?" I ask as kindly as I can.

SHE OFFERS A SHAKY SMILE. "I'm not sure that guy liked me very much."

I SCOFF, trying to show her it's all right. "He's just an old man who didn't like having his sleep disturbed. It'll be okay. We'll be out of his hair in the morning anyway, and he's getting three times what the room is worth for bothering with us."

. . .

"Okay," she mumbles, looking around and then quietly taking off my jacket and her "borrowed" lab coat. Now that she's had time on the road and a meal in her, she looks less like a Japanese ghost and more cute and artsy. A college girl—startlingly normal.

The truth is, I don't like how the owner looked at us either. Like he assumes I'm a married man having an affair, or that we are some drunken late-night bar hookup. I don't actually care about his angry, conservative disapproval. People like that need to keep their noses out.

"So you never told me much about yourself," she prods so gently that I barely mind. "I know what you do for a living but really, nothing else. What do you do when you're not working?"

I let out a rueful little laugh. "Well, I don't actually have all that much free time right now. See, I inherited a big administrative mess from my predecessor, so I give up part of every week finishing up all the paperwork he left."

"That must be hard on whoever's special in your life," she observes, so softly that I know she's feeling wistful about filling that position. *She's got a crush. Okay. That's kind of adorable.*

. . .

"Heh, no, not really," I say with an awkwardness I'm not accustomed to. "My staff feed my pets when I'm gone."

Her face lights up, and I brace myself for the standard gold-digger refrain: "You have staff?" Meaning, of course, that I make enough money to *afford* staff.

But instead, she squeaks, "You have pets?"

I fight down a huge grin. *Okay, that's definitely adorable.* "Yeah. Two rescue dogs—a Pit-Rottie mix named Smiley and a standard-issue brown mutt named Jake. Plus Derp; he's the cat. Black and white, kinda ... special." I grab the one chair in the room, a stiff wooden rocker, and stretch my legs out in front of me.

She blinks as she takes a seat on the edge of the bed. "Special how?" she asks in that strange innocent tone.

"Well, he knows all the usual tricks of feeding and cleaning himself, uses the litter box, doesn't wander into traffic. He just happens to, uh ... think he's a dog." That is actually kind of an understatement.

"Wait." She leans forward a little, and I try to avoid staring into the sweater's overlarge neckline. "You mean that he plays fetch?"

. . .

"Yep. He prefers socks or small chewy bones."

"He uses chewy bones." She's relaxing now, intrigued.

Behold the power of cute animals. "Yeah, and God help the skin on your hands if you try to take it away."

"Does he bark?"

I shake my head, smiling, my relief probably showing on my face. The further we get from that hospital, the more she acts like a normal person. Yes, she might be a bit mousy, tense, and socially inexperienced, but she's getting less depressed, less skittish and less ... broken.

She's a really special girl, this one. She needs a lot of help, but as things go on, I'm starting to feel like I wouldn't mind. I look after people all the time. Why would I balk at looking after my woman?

"You're ... staring at me," she murmurs wonderingly.

I look at her and make myself a promise. No matter how hard it is, I'm going to be completely honest with her and let her decide how to act on the information. And that's how we'll handle it from now on.

. . .

"I'm sorry, I just ... you've changed so much just in a few hours." Has she been faking everything amazingly well? Am I that gullible? Or is she actually improving now that she is off the psych meds?

If she needs tranquilizers, her mood should not be improving. I could be wrong—she could just be on a temporary emotional high from finally getting free of her captor. But that's certainly not how it seems. "It's like you're becoming more ... alive."

"The poison's starting to wear off." Her face is thoughtful; her expressions have become more animated as well, helping her shed more of that ghostly look. "That and just ... being free, and finally being around someone I actually want to be around."

"Well, I'm sure glad you feel that way." I stare at her, trying to look ambivalent, not sure whether to bring up my desire or wait.

"What is it?" She looks at me in confusion, and I smile a little awkwardly.

That's okay. I don't have to be smooth. She's rough edged and inexperienced and probably will feel better if I show that I'm not perfect either. "Well, it's just that I've been thinking of kissing you for a while now, but I know you're coming out of a bad situation."

. . .

WHEN DID I GET UP? I barely notice until I'm settling onto the bed next to her. My cock is throbbing almost painfully in my pants, and I reach over and lay one hand gently over hers.

SHE SHIVERS, but her eyes light up. "Oh," she murmurs. "I ... don't have any experience with that kind of thing."

HER TONE IS UNCERTAIN, and for a moment I'm concerned enough that I almost call the whole thing off. I don't want to scare her or do anything that might leave her with more pain and me with any guilt.

"IS THAT OKAY?" she's asking, and for a few beats, I stare at her in confusion.

"I'M SORRY, WHAT?"

"THAT I DON'T KNOW what I'm doing," she clarifies, looking nervous and embarrassed, and maybe even a little apologetic.

"HUH? OH, NO, NO. SERIOUSLY." I give her hand a squeeze. "Nobody knows what they are doing in the beginning when it comes to sex."

"I JUST DON'T WANT to embarrass myself, or ... or make you angry." Her shy glance breaks my heart a little.

. . .

"You're not going to make me angry," I reassure gently. "Yes, intervening in a suicide is a really weird way to meet people, but I think you're sweet and attractive. It's not why I decided to help you, but it is the reason I want to kiss you."

"Oh," she says with that tiny, tentative smile again. "O ... okay."

My heart starts beating fast and I turn toward her, licking my lips. "Yeah?" I double check.

"Yeah," she replies, holding my hand in both of hers.

CHAPTER 8

Madelyne

First kiss. Another thing I thought I would never experience. Aaron's lips are warm and wide and firm against mine, and a tingle shoots from my lips back through my whole body, like sparks being struck between us.

WHATEVER ELSE HAPPENS, *whether I'm caught, whether I die, at least I'll have this,* I think feverishly as I respond. My return kiss is a little breathy and clumsy, but he seems to enjoy it anyway. We hold each other tight and kiss and breathe each other in until I'm dizzy from it.

ALL THOSE LONELY, terrifying years in the doctor's hands left me with no real idea what affection is. I hadn't known it well enough to recognize what I've been starving for. Just a hug, a kiss, Aaron's hand stroking my hair—it fills up empty places inside of me that I wasn't aware of. "Interesting," he murmurs thoughtfully, and keeps caressing me until his own breathing shivers and grows harsh.

He pulls off his button-down shirt, startling me with how heavily muscled he is beneath. His body is tanned, gold hairs gleaming on his forearms and in a trail down his lower belly. Tossing the cloth aside and kicking off his shoes, he clambers onto the bed and moves around behind me on his knees.

I AM BUSYING myself kicking off the white nursing slip-ons when I feel him move up behind me, brushing my hair away from the back of my neck. Then his lips come down on my nape and I gasp, my newly-bared toes curling.

HE HOLDS ME FROM BEHIND, pushing up the tank top to bare my back while I shiver and pant in his grip. His mouth refastens on my neck, nipping and licking, then moving slowly downward. I tremble, nails digging into my knees, low moans pushing out of me with every breath.

I AM STARTING to crave his bare skin against mine—our whole bodies, tangled together. I have no idea exactly what it will feel like to have the cock I feel pressed against me inside of me instead. But I want every inch of it, even if it hurts.

HIS LIPS and tongue run up and down my spine, lowering gradually toward my hips. I whimper and gasp, my pussy starting to ache in an unfamiliar way that feels good and drives me crazy at the same time.

THE DOCTOR WOULD ACTUALLY SHOW anger if he saw me like this —free, clearheaded, emotional, sexual. It's all the more reason to throw myself into it now that I've found someone right. Impatient, brave, defiant, I strip off the tank top altogether, and take the plain bra beneath with it.

AARON LETS OUT A STARTLED CHUCKLE, and then his hands slide around my ribcage and move up under my breasts. He teases me with his fingertips, just brushing against the undersides before cupping them warmly in each of his smooth palms. His hands are steady and sure, and my small breasts disappear completely under his palms, even as the brush of his skin against my nipples sends fresh pleasure through me.

I CAN'T SEEM to get my breath at all anymore. I'm not worried— the strange, lightheaded sensation exhilarates me. He wraps his arms around me and scoots me back with him, then shifts our positions and lays me back sideways across his lap.

I can feel his throbbing cock push against me through the crotch of his pants. He leans down and kisses me, then runs his mouth down my neck, suckling lingeringly at my pulse. When I'm starting to breathe heavily again, his mouth continues its trek and he runs the tip of his tongue down my skin toward my breast.

. . .

I FEEL faint as he sucks my nipple into his mouth, my head falling back and a shuddering moan escaping me. He keeps suckling gently, stroking my other nipple with his fingertips. My eyes close and I lose track of time, barely aware of anything beyond pleasure as he starts tugging at my skirt.

I LIFT my hips and pull the heavy velvet off, taking my plain panties with them. It's brazen—risky—and I peek at him, shivering. He smiles against my breast and starts stroking my belly in circles with his free hand, slowly moving downward.

WHEN HIS FINGERS start caressing my pussy the sensations double, making all my muscles shake and tighten. A wild sense of anticipation fills me. Then he slips two of his fingers in between the top of my pussy lips and starts to delicately stroke.

MY VOICE GOES HOARSE, low, purring moans vibrating my throat as my hips roll in time with his sucking lips and stroking fingers. I can feel something building fast in my core, my whole body feeling like it's tightening up as I pant and gasp and struggle to beg for more. "Please ..."

"SHHHHH," he rumbles softly and moves away just enough that he can shuck off his pants and underwear. I roll over to watch—and stare at the huge tool that he frees from his fly. I don't have much experience with cocks, but this one is hefty and long—a little intimidating, in fact. My breath catches and my eyes widen slightly as I wonder how this is going to go.

. . .

His eyes gleam with amusement and desire as he catches my expression. "Just relax," he purrs, as my whole body trembles on the edge of something. He is pulling me back onto his lap, facing him this time, as he spreads his thighs.

He props my legs apart against his chest and takes his cock in his hand, his eyes locked on mine. I feel the head of his erection against my lower lips and take a deep breath, bracing myself.

The silky head parts my tight, tingling flesh and slides into my cunt, slow and easy, as my fingers curl against the bedspread. He pants through his teeth, his breath shuddering, and pushes on until his cock is completely inside of me. Then, pinning my legs against his chest and shoulders with one arm, he reaches down and starts stroking me again.

My head falls back and lolls from side to side against the bedspread. When I manage to look up, I see him looming over me, belly flexing magnificently as his cock disappears into me over and over again.

It doesn't hurt. Not really. The little edge of pain just gives the pleasure teeth. I claw at the bedspread, writhing, hungry, needing ... *something*.

He speeds up, lips parting and eyes closed, low, rumbling groans bursting out of him every time our hips meet. His fingers never waver in their caresses. And suddenly, it becomes urgent that they don't.

My body gathers as if to leap somewhere, every muscle tightening and drawing up, my mind blurring. And then—

I hear my cries as he grinds against me and my muscles clench around him in waves. Ecstasy bursts through me again and again—and as I'm reaching my absolute peak I hear him shout with pleasure. We're grinding against each other now, and suddenly I feel his cock start to spasm.

I look up at him, his back arched, head thrown back, his chest heaving as his cock jolts and releases a hot rush inside me. I hear him groan with joy a last time ... and then his head droops over me and he sighs with contentment.

We have to catch our breath before we gain the strength to disentangle. I curl on my side, skin tingling, body loose, astonished. After a few moments, he curls up behind me and tugs me back against him.

I doze. Sometimes I wake up suddenly, disoriented, and look around the room before his breath blows warm on my nape and his arms tighten a little around me. It makes me feel safe, and I drift off again.

. . .

At least, no matter what happens, I will have this to look back on, I repeat to myself over and over again as I fall asleep.

CHAPTER 9

Aaron

We make love twice more before I finally wear her out, and then I watch her sleep. She looks so innocent and relaxed, her long lashes resting against her cheek and her breathing gone soft and slow. The scars on her wrists tell a story that I hope she will never have to revisit again, and the love bites on her and the scratches on me tell a story I hope she will remember fondly.

I know now that I want to keep her in my life, but until her captor is caught, that might be ... problematic. She doesn't want to be anywhere close to the area where I live and work, and I can't just walk away from my life. But I can't walk away from her either.

There's so much we don't know about each other—so much that I want to know, and want her to know too. I want to see how she is when she has healed. When she feels better and isn't constantly afraid of being sent back to *that place*.

And of course, I want to get whoever did this to her put away.

I don't want him to get away with this, and I don't want him to get a chance to do it to anyone else.

I sleep for a while as the sky lightens. When there is enough light to see by, I sigh and get up, heading for the bathroom. I'll shower off, get dressed, find us something for breakfast, and then wake Madelyne with it. Then we had better get moving.

As it turns out, everything goes as planned until I'm getting dressed and glance out the window—just as two cop cars pull into the parking lot. I watch them as they slow—and then see the old man running out in his goddamned housecoat to get their attention.

"What the hell?" I mutter, feeling a surge of apprehension. I look back at Madelyne. It might not have anything to do with either of us but ... "Maddy, baby, wake up. You need to get dressed. We're leaving."

Running from the police has never been on my radar for this trip. I watch as she opens her eyes and sits up instantly, looking around disoriented. I start helping her into her clothes while she blinks up at me, like she's starting to realize that neither last night nor this rude awakening was a dream.

She scrambles into her clothes as soon as she can, and I give the room a once-over before we walk out the door. She doesn't ask me what it is, but her face is white and she's very quiet. Her eyes are full of terror.

I remember what she claimed about the local police being wrapped around her captor's finger. I had dismissed it as paranoia or fearful ramblings, but right now I know she has some reason to fear the cops wherever she goes. But ... is it the reason that she gave me, or is something else going on?

"I don't know why the police are here, but we should leave. You don't need the drama, and I don't need the delays." I push open the door to the back stairwell—and nearly run into a burly black cop with a bemused look on his face.

Madelyne lets out a squeak of dismay and I reach back to grip her hand. "It's okay," I try to tell her, though really I have no idea whether it is or not. I make eye contact with the cop. "Sorry, Officer."

"That's no problem," he says in a deep, calm voice. Then he looks down at a photograph in his hand ... and up at Madelyne. His deep brown eyes narrow.

"Madelyne Deacon, I'm going to need you to come with me," he says in an emotionless, authoritative tone.

"What the hell—?" I start—and then Madelyne takes off with a cry of horror and starts running down the hallway so fast she leaves one of her outsized shoes behind.

The cop pushes past me and chases after her, calling "Miss Deacon! We're not going to hurt you! We just need to return you to the hospital! You're not well!"

I freeze, and my heart sinks into my shoes.

How's this for a news headline? Escaped mental patient cons clueless, horny doctor into aiding her in escaping from an involuntary hold. She is a danger to herself and others, but in a misguided attempt to help her regain her lust for life, he crosses state lines with her and even ends up fucking her. He doesn't even realize that he's being manipulated and used until the police show up on their doorstep.

It's ironic. She told me the truth in many ways. Held against her will, drugged, abandoned ... the common lot of psychotic people. All she wants is to be free. I gave her that for a little while, and she was happy. But that's not a cure for psychosis.

I should have known when I figured out that other pill was Seroquel. It's anti-anxiety, yes, but it's mostly used as an anti-psychotic. Feeling like the biggest idiot in the world, I watch as two cops emerge from the far stairwell and catch the sobbing, struggling Madelyne in a firm grip.

"Aaron! Don't let them take me!" she calls in anguish, and I feel my throat choke up with shame. *She trusted me. But I can't do anything!* "Please, please don't let them take me back to that place!"

I move forward. "Officers, please, what's going on?"

"Just stay back, sir," the first one snaps in a voice of cold authority. "This woman is an escaped mental patient. We need you at the station for questioning, and in return we'll answer all your questions there."

"Officer, wait, please. There may be more to this story than the doctor caring for her has told you." It is a long shot, trying to appeal to their empathy, but it gives all three of them pause, and they turn to look at me.

"I'm a medical doctor. This woman reports excessive tranquilization and has scars on her wrists and ankles from excessive and improper use of restraints. There may be abuses going on at the facility where she is being held. It might not be safe to return her to that environment."

The first cop stares at me thoughtfully while Madelyne sobs behind him, each of her arms held by a bored-looking female cop. Then he nods once. "Be that as it may, our hands are as tied as yours are. And according to her doctor, the restraints are needed. She's reported to have bitten her stepfather severely."

"That's because he tried to rape me! I was ten! Dear God, why do you listen to the doctor and not me?" Tears stream down her face as she pleads with the police. It hurts to watch.

"Even if what you're saying is true, doctor," the man says smoothly as he turns back to me. Over his shoulder I can see them cuffing Madelyne while she pleads for them to stop. "You'll have to talk to the local medical board, and maybe help her to retain a lawyer."

"I don't even know the name of her doctor," I start to protest —and then I close my mouth. *Yes, I do.*

It all fits. The abuses, the overuse of drugs and restraints, the mix of arrogance and incompetence. Not to mention where I found Madelyne.

It's Dr. Westridge.

"May I talk to her before you take her away?" I ask as calmly as I can.

"No, that's not a good idea." His smile is tight, and I stare at him in disbelief.

"Please, I just need to reassure her." I move forward, but he steps in front of me again.

"Doctor, you need to know how bad this looks right now. You were caught assisting a fugitive from involuntary care in crossing state lines. Now, I'm willing to cut you a break, but it depends on your cooperation." He stares me firmly in the eyes, and I hitch in a breath and nod.

Shit.

I look past him at Madelyne, and our eyes meet. She's terrified, but resigned as well. She can see the cop keeping me from running to her rescue this time, and with tears in her eyes, she swallows and nods.

"Don't give up," I call out to her. "I'll find a way to help!"

Then they take her away, and a piece of my heart feels like it rips clean out of my chest and goes chasing after her.

I don't know what to believe. She's an escaped mental patient. But she may be being abused. She also may be being held illegally. Misdiagnosed, overmedicated. By a guy I already despise.

"Can I follow you in my car?" I ask the officer in a tired voice.

"That's fine."

The interview takes two hours, and by the end of it, I swear the cop, whose name is James Adams, almost feels sorry for me. Not because I'm a sap who was pulled in by a sad story and came very close to breaking several laws—though that is true. But rather because by the time we shake hands and I walk out to my car, he knows the kind of fight I have ahead of me.

"Miss Deacon's juvenile records are sealed except for incidents related to her psych diagnosis. Normally we have to wait for signed permission for medical records, but her doctor just handed us a copy. Yeah, that's probably a privacy violation.

"Born to Linda and Hiro Deacon of Marin County, she showed no behavioral problems until after her father's sudden death when she was six. Linda almost immediately remarried to a Peter Sanders and Madelyne's violent outbursts started five months after that.

"The girl complained of inappropriate touching by Sanders to a daycare worker, who called the police. Her parents immediately pulled her out of that daycare and the investigation turned up inconclusive. After that, incidents of Madelyne becoming violent toward Sanders happened at least twice a week."

I get on my motorcycle and sit there, feeling an ache run through me that there's no small, warm body and slim set of arms pressed against me now. *I would have taken her anywhere,* I think sadly. I still want to. But now there is all this shit in the way.

"Madelyne always claimed that she was protecting herself from Sanders trying to molest her, but there was never any evidence, and her mother always took Sanders' side. When Madelyne was ten, Linda threw her daughter out of the house due to her ongoing feud with Sanders. Madelyne responded by running into traffic on a nearby highway."

The engine roars to life and I take off down the highway toward home, a new determination growing in my heart.

"She was committed to the inpatient mental health program at Ravenwood Hospital, where she has remained in the care of Dr. Emmanuel Westridge ever since. No violent incidents have been reported, but Madelyne has now been legally abandoned by her mother.

"Dr. Westridge has deemed her a perpetual danger to herself and others."

I think back on last night—on her terror and resilience, on the beauty in her face as she found her smile, of her body trembling in my arms as we found ecstasy together. "Dr. Westridge is full of shit," I growl to myself as the Harley roars along. "And I'm going to prove it."

CHAPTER 10

Madelyne

"I just don't know what I'm going to do with you, young lady," Dr. Westridge chides, his sugar-coated Georgia accent dripping with long-suffering disdain. "You know you're not safe in the outside world. How far did you really think that you were going to get?"

I stare at him mutely from inside a cocoon of drugs so thick that I can barely move. I'm in a wheelchair, my calves and forearms bound snugly to it, and I can barely keep my eyes open. I suppose it's better than the complete breakdown that came before, but not by much.

The doctor is in a white suit today, with a narrow black tie and too many rings. His pale, bald head shines like he polishes it, distracting from the small round spectacles that frame his colorless little eyes. He smiles too much—tiny, nasty little smiles, flashing small white teeth or just smugly curling up at the corners.

"Well, never mind. The point is, you're back now, and it's

time for you to return to your care regimen." He removes his spectacles and starts polishing the lenses. "Any questions?"

My chin is wet. My cheeks burn with humiliation, but I can't even make myself stop drooling, let alone actually speak. I wonder if he knows it, or if he's so caught up in his own craziness that he imagines me talking anyway.

Aaron promised he'd get me out of this. But he also promised he would get me safely away. He saved me twice ... but when the third time came, he failed. He barely even tried.

I know it's not rational to expect him to go up against the police, but now, back in my hell, with my own smiling devil walking around and around me while he looks me over, I wish Aaron had tried.

Except, maybe he is trying. Maybe he's out there in the world of medical boards and lawyers and things that good doctors use to get things done. Maybe he will save me, after all.

Time starts to wear on. It's getting cooler outside. Sometimes dead leaves blow past my window. I think they drug and restrain me for a week, maybe two. Immobile and tended to, I'm helpless as a baby.

By the time cardboard turkeys replace the skeletons at the nursing station, they have me swallowing pills again instead of taking injections, and shuffling around on my own. I feel weak and drained inside and say little to anyone, giving every appearance of having gone back to doing everything I'm told.

I'm biding my time. And meanwhile, I'm weaning off of my own damn medication in secret. I refuse to be drugged any more.

I hide the pills inside the hollow knob that is used as a drawer pull in my bedside table. Just one pill a day at first. Then two. I probably should just flush them. I should have faith that Aaron's coming for me, and that my Plan B will never be needed.

But he might just decide that I'm a crazy girl who tricked

him, and that I should be locked away. And if he does think that, I can expect no other help from anyone. And that's where my Plan B comes in.

I don't want to end like this. I don't want to be another sad suicide in a nut house, who no one will ever remember. But can I trust Aaron to get me out? As time keeps crawling on, the knob fills up with pills, and the turkey decorations get taken down, and I wonder if he's forgotten about me.

One dark, despairing night, I lie in my bed in tears, staring up at the moon and wondering why I haven't even heard from Aaron at all. I take the knob off the drawer and shake the pills out into my palm. There are a lot of them now. More than enough.

I stare at them for a very long time.

The doctor doesn't want me dead. It will make him look bad. My mother doesn't want me dead. My suicide will open the can of worms that will lead to an investigation.

Aaron doesn't want me dead. But where is he? Why hasn't he done anything?

After a long time of sitting still while a war goes on inside my heart, I pour the pills back into the knob and screw it back onto the drawer. There's another way to get my revenge besides dying tragically and letting the press see the blood in the water. And that is to fight.

But I'll need Aaron's help to do that.

"Hurry up," I murmur at the ceiling, still clinging to hope by my nails.

CHAPTER 11

Aaron

It takes two months of fighting before I come for Madelyne. Two months of phone calls to the medical board, talking to the hospital directors, pointing out the discrepancies between her diagnoses and the medications she is on, and requesting an examination for signs of abuse.

Two months of pulling together a legal team, leaning on the board, and talking to anyone who could help me make a case. Her pediatrician. Cops involved in the case. Even, in a moment of desperation, her mother—who slams the phone down as soon as I say what I am calling about.

The hospital Christmas tree is up and all the leaves have fallen off the maples on the day that I walk in the door of the psychiatric wing of Ravenwood with a team of three lawyers. Staff members see me coming and their eyes widen. One of them scurries to page Westridge.

"Dr. Stokes! What a pleasant surprise." Westridge sweeps toward me down the hall after a few minutes ... only to slow, his smile fading, when he sees the lawyers and the sheaf of papers in my hand. "How may I be of assistance to you?"

"You can immediately prepare Madelyne Deacon for discharge," I say coldly, handing over the first few papers. "Her care is by necessity being transferred to another facility." Namely, an outpatient program at a very good clinic down the coast.

He pales so suddenly that it makes my skin crawl a little. Is he that desperate to keep controlling her? "By necessity? I'm sorry?"

One of the lawyers, Jamison, steps forward, coughing into his bony fist. "No police reports, incident statements, or witness statements exist to verify your claim that this client must be held in perpetuity against her will. We are obliged to inform you that an investigation into Miss Deacon's care is ongoing, as is a general investigation of your fitness to remain director of this facility."

Westridge turns from white to red. "How dare you imply—"

"No one is implying anything. The investigation is a matter of record." I step forward and look him in the eye. "As is the emergency order of protection that bans you from being within one thousand feet of her until the conclusion of this investigation."

His eyes widen in horror—it's the most satisfying sight I have seen in a long time. A round, curly-haired brunette nurse approaches as he's standing there spluttering. "Doctor?" she asks me tentatively.

"She'll need some help filling out her discharge paperwork," I say, and offer the nurse the shopping bag in my other hand. "I brought her some clothes and shoes."

The smile the nurse shoots me is full of relief. But a moment later she flinches as Westridge goes rocketing over the edge.

His face has gone from red to purple. "No, you don't do any

such thing, missy, don't you dare! I run this hospital, and I call the shots!" His hands and voice both shake. It's like some kind of explosion is building up.

I calmly get between him and the reedy lawyer and startled nurse. "Not this time."

The nurse goes to do her job, taking the bag with her. I stare down Westridge, who glares at me like an infant on the verge of a tantrum.

"You ... you ... you're only doing this because you've had it in for me since the beginning! That girl is crazy! She needs my control to survive! She needs me!"

"You're the last thing she needs," I spit in disgust.

By the time that Madelyne comes walking down the hall in her new blue dress, her eyes lighting up as she sees me, Westridge has gone from yelling to trying to hit me with a medicine tray. I sidestep him, and several orderlies grab him.

Madelyne walks up beside me and watches as they drag a screeching, plum-faced Westridge to where one of the desk nurses is preparing a sedative. Her eyes search my face; I smile at her. She takes my hand with a look of relief, and we watch as a whining, mumbling Westridge is bundled into a wheelchair and wheeled away.

"You came back," she says in soft wonder, and I smile and slip an arm around her.

"I said I would. I'm just sorry that it took so long. But I hope this counts as a good apology—and a halfway decent Christmas present." I wink at her, and her smile blooms again despite everything.

She leans her head against me. "It's the best Christmas present." She's still in a bit of a drug-induced haze, but she doesn't seem half as bad as that life-changing night I found her on the bridge.

We watch until Westridge is gone, and then go to the desk to sort out Maddy's discharge. The rest of the staff seems relieved at the turn of events, and several wish her well as we go.

I shake hands with the lawyers. "The board will need copies of everything. Please see to it, and I'll call you when I need to move forward on the permanent protection order." Though after today, if I'm lucky, Westridge will be declared unfit.

Once Madelyne and I are standing alone outside the hospital, she turns to me and we hug each other tight. "Thank you," she says softly.

"You're welcome. So ... where do you want to go from here?" I brush my fingertips down her cheek. There's a smell of rain in the chilly air, but I don't mind. A cold ride will be warmer with her arms around me.

Her eyes light up. "Did you bring the motorcycle?"

"I did." I gesture toward the Harley. "You ... want to head north again for the weekend? I could book us a suite in Portland."

"Absolutely." The light in her eyes is amazing, as if I've rekindled all her hopes at once. Once we reach the motorcycle, she kisses me, and then hops on the back. "Let's ride."

The End.

SIGN UP TO RECEIVE FREE BOOKS

Sign Up to Receive Free E-Books and Audiobook Codes.

Would you like to read **The Unexpected Nanny, Dirty Little Virgin** and **other romance books** for **free**?

You can sign up to receive these free e-books and audiobooks by typing this link into your browser:

https://www.steamyromance.info/free-books-and-audiobooks-hot-and-steamy/

Or this one:

https://www.steamyromance.info/the-unexpected-nanny-free/

PREVIEW OF HOME IS WHERE THE HEAT IS
A SECRET BABY CHRISTMAS ROMANCE

By Michelle Love

Blurb

"My life was finally where I wanted it to be ... or was it?"

The price was my family, my hometown, and my reputation but my musical career was finally panning out. Unfortunately, the universe had other plans for my brother and me, taking me back from LA to Alpena, Michigan.
I would not have gotten far without Leila Butler, my brother Micah making no secret how he loathed me. If it wasn't for the sexy, sweet blonde and her amazing way with him, who knew where I'd be?
Probably back in LA where I belonged.

"I'd held onto my virginity long enough to lose it to the most unlikely candidate—a wander-lusting bad boy with no desire to stay put."

And I knew better too. Everyone knew that Jayce Joyce was selfish—he left his family behind, hoping to find himself in Los Angeles.

Had he always been this gorgeous? Maybe I was starstruck. Was that why I couldn't decline when he offered me a job watching over the house and Micah?

I really wanted to watch over him.

Yet, right from the start, I knew his heart didn't really belong to me—the music was claiming him again, just as it had before.

How could a small-time girl like me compete with the glitz and glamour of LA?

PROLOGUE

JAYCE

When I was about four or five, I remember telling my dad I wanted a little brother. Even then, he looked at me with hauntingly chocolate eyes and shook his head like I had asked him for both of his kidneys.

"It's not in the cards, Jason," he declared in the same tone he used when I asked for another serving of ice cream for dessert. "Just not in the cards."

It took me a few years to understand why he looked at me like that—the fact he and my mom were teenagers when they had me and my request had come when he was a twenty-one-year-old high school dropout, working for pennies as a farmhand while my mom cleaned hotel rooms in our little town of Alpena, Michigan.

Reflecting back on those years, I don't remember having a need—there was always food on the table, even if it was KD three nights out of seven. I had my own room as well, even if it was the size of the walk-in closet at my place in Los Angeles. It actually may have been smaller—I never measured. In retrospect, having to share that space was not pleasant for anyone—four people in a two-bedroom trailer wasn't exactly opulence.

Three people were bad enough. Not that I had a concept of what the high life was back then.

It didn't help that I was not the most obedient child, a trait that didn't improve with maturity. I guess it took a couple of decades for the bitter memory of raising me to wear off before they tried again.

Too bad my parents didn't anticipate they could possibly have a worse kid than me, especially not in their forties. Or maybe it was better they were older—they say the older you get, the less you care. I never found that to be true. Of course, I wasn't in my forties.

Nevertheless, Micah was a bigger shithead than I ever was, even if I say so myself.

I was thinking of this as I smirked at my parents. Sitting in my spot across from my younger brother, I was watching his abhorrent table manners with my peripheral vision. I would never have gotten away with that when I was his age. Dad would have given me a single backhand to the head and I would have sat up and used my knife. Or even just "the look." Whatever happened to "the look"? Kids nowadays get away with murder.

"Just because we're poor, Jason, doesn't mean you have to act like an animal!" Dad would chant in my ear so much, I would hear it in my dreams. I guess the same rules didn't apply for Micah.

There was a decided contrast in the dining room that night. Mom had gone all out again, decorating for the season, the fading white string lights and low-playing Christmas tunes in the background, the seven-foot real pine emanating an overpowering aroma as it sparkled with glass bulbs and tinsel garlands. Presents were already all over the floor even though the 25th was two days away. None of that, not even the crackling wood of the fireplace in the living room, could overpower the unspoken tension looming over our small family, sucking the air from the room.

"So, Jason, honey," my mom, Beth, cooed in her soft, maternal way. "How's the singing?"

My half smile quickly faded; my eyes darting toward her scowling.

"*My singing?*" I echoed in disbelief. "*How's my singing?*"

It never ceased to amaze me how easily disdain arose.

"Watch your tone, Jason," Dad snapped without looking up from his roast beef. He was on autopilot, ready to verbally reprimand me like in childhood.

Oh sure, but you can't see your youngest shoveling peas into his mouth like a zombie apocalypse is at the door, right?

"I'm sorry, baby," Mom sighed. "Did I offend you?"

She sounded exhausted; no surprise. Things had gotten decidedly better for my parents, specifically after I'd moved from Michigan and pursued my career in Los Angeles.

Gone was the shitty trailer in Greenhaven Community Park. I didn't know how that hunk of metal had survived as long as it had. Nowadays my parents lived in a quaint two-story abode on the outskirts of Alpena. Dad wasn't toiling on someone else's farm, not since the app he'd developed went viral. Who knew people could make money creating apps? But Mom? She seemed tired, despite the fact she hadn't worked since Micah was born. Handling that kid was worse than cleaning toilets. Or maybe she was weary of life. My dad was a prick sometimes. Since childhood, I hadn't been able to imagine why she'd married him.

This was the first time I had been home in three years and it was already regretful, even though, admittedly, eating Mom's concoctions was better than I remembered. Between recording sessions, I didn't get a lot of pot roast at all.

"My *singing* is great, Mom," I grunted, tossing my fork on the table and running a hand through my wavy black hair. It was getting long, but my agent, Daryn, told me to leave it, that women loved the "rock-star" look. Yup, her name was Daryn, but in LA everyone was graced with ridiculous names, I had quickly learned. I had no idea what was their birthright and which were monikers and had stopped asking long ago.

"Don't you have a song or something?" Micah piped up, his mouth bursting with potatoes.

"Micah," Mom chided tenderly. "Don't speak with your mouth full."

My brother ignored her and kept his dark eyes focused on me. He looked like Dad, like us. We all had the same jet-black hair and intense brown eyes. My poor mom's recessive blonde genes didn't stand a chance. Dad had told me once that there was native blood four generations back or something. I'd always maintained the school of thought that we were all mixed with something after thousands of years of war, but that's another story.

"Well? Don't you?" Micah insisted, and it annoyed me. I might have been a brat, but never that rude. Meaningfully, I looked at my father, wondering if he would rein in his youngest, but he seemed oblivious.

The baby really gets away with everything!

"I have a few *songs*," I retorted. "My latest single is climbing the charts."

I told my family about my success. Leaving Alpena had been the best decision—there was absolutely nothing for me in that one-horse town. Although I should have done it sooner.

"Yeah. I think one of my teachers likes your music," Micah said, turning his attention back to his meal. It stung me that my own brother didn't care if I made it huge in the music industry. Against all odds, a poor-ass kid from Nowhere, Michigan, had made his way into the daunting world of rock and here was my punk-ass brother, making me feel like a nobody.

I shouldn't have come home, Christmas or not. I shouldn't have succumbed to my mom's wistful emails and guilt trips. They'd asked me to visit to make me feel like shit.

And they'd succeeded. Again.

"That's wonderful, honey," Mom said, likely sensing my rising frustration. "I'll have to pick up your CD."

Micah and I both guffawed.

"CD?" we chorused, exchanging a look. Mom looked embarrassed.

"Isn't that how we listen to music?"

Micah giggled, and I couldn't help but grin at her dated views but simultaneously gave her credit for making an effort. My dad had barely uttered a coherent sentence since I'd arrived the previous day. He was still pissed about my going off on my own shortly after Micah was born, and he was not proud of my choices.

I was waiting for the lid on his top to blow.

"So that's it?" Dad said suddenly, raising his head for the first time. "You'll continue to chase this juvenile fantasy?"

My back stiffened.

There it is. It didn't take him long.

"Gary ..." Mom gave my father a warning look but it was too late. He was there. To his credit, he probably had held out as long as he could.

"Fantasy? Making six figures a year is not a fantasy."

Dad stared at me, the contempt on his face unmasked. It was hard to believe we were only seventeen years apart. He was like an old man to me, even in adulthood, even at the age of thirty. In LA, I had friends his age but they were nothing like this judgmental, glowering bear that looked at me as if he'd caught me skipping class.

No matter how successful I become, I'll always be the same kid to him.

"And what? You're going to be like Keith Richards?" he insisted, disdain in his voice. "Is that what you think? You'll play rock and roll until you're dead?"

That's ridiculous. Keith Richards will never die. He's a vampire or something.

"GARY!"

"What, Beth? He's thirty years old. He's chased this stupid dream long enough. It's one thing to encourage his creativity and quite another to guide him into homelessness."

"You're homeless?" Micah asked, his eyes widening. "Cool!"

"NOT COOL!" both my parents yelled in unison.

I rose from the table, steeling my shaking hands. It always caught me off guard when he confronted me like that. I loathed myself for letting him getting under my skin again. That was why I'd stayed away for so long.

"Thanks for dinner, Mom." I coldly tossed my napkin on the table. "I'm going to bed and leaving in the morning."

I didn't give her a chance to respond and stormed away from the table.

"JASON!" she cried after me. "Gary! Go after him. It's Christmas, for God's sake! He hasn't been home in years!"

But it wouldn't matter what he said. Even if he apologized, he thought I was a failure. It didn't matter that I was so close to a contract with a real label. He'd scoff and ask how many times he'd heard that before.

I wasn't sitting through it. I'd come too far, struggled too hard to be mocked by my own family.

Falling on the bed in the guest bedroom (which had once been my room for a brief time) I stared at the ceiling and tried to steady my nerves.

I'll catch the first flight back to LA and won't come back until he's dead.

The thought shamed me but before I could justify it, there was a knock at the door.

"I don't want to hear it!" The door opened anyhow and Micah appeared.

"Are you really leaving tomorrow?" he asked from the threshold. He'd traded his dinner for a piece of chocolate cake which he stabbed with a fork as he spoke. Life continued when I was gone.

No one batted an eye. They just pulled out the cake. Maybe that's why they pulled out the cake—in celebration.

"Yep." More guilt. It wasn't Micah's fault I was angry. He might have a little snot, but he was only six years old and I didn't know him at all. Thanks to Dad, my brother was a stranger to me.

"You can come visit me in LA," I told him, softening my tone. "I'm sure Mom would bring you."

His eyebrows shot up as he chewed on his cake deliberately, watching me with curious eyes. It took him a long while to swallow.

"Why?" he finally asked.

"Why what? There's tons to do."

"Why would I come and visit *you*?"

I felt heat warming my cheeks.

"Why not? We're brothers, you know."

Micah shrugged.

"I guess." He stuffed another forkful of icing into his mouth. This time he didn't wait until his mouth was clear before speaking. "I don't really know you."

My neck was so tense it was going to snap.

"We could change that. We could hang out and ... stuff."

That sounded so lame but I didn't know how to talk to this kid. He was absolutely correct. We shared blood, but that was it.

And if I don't make an effort, that's all we'll ever be—strangers who share blood.

"What do you say?" I pressed when he didn't respond. "Will you come visit?"

He shook his head.

"I don't think so," he replied, turning away.

"Wait! Why not?"

He glanced at me and sighed.

"Because things are ... heavy. You make things ... I dunno ... harder."

He was gone, leaving me processing what he said.

A full-grown man had been dismissed by a six-year-old and reprimanded by his father.

I sat up and began packing my suitcase, determined to leave tonight. I didn't need this. I was just fine in California without them.

Why did I suppose having a brother was a good idea? I gritted my teeth.

I called a cab and proceeded to Alpena County Regional Airport with only one phrase ringing in my mind with sheer resolve.

It will be too soon if I see them again. I don't need them.

And I meant it ... at the time.

CHAPTER ONE

Jayce

In the recording studio, the headphones canceled out the sounds around me as I poured my soul into the microphone, my eyes firmly closed. I was caught up in the melody flowing from my lips and into the track.

It was the same when I finished a song I'd sweated over; the all-nighters perfecting the lyrics, the bickering with bandmates, self-deprecation—all worthwhile. I wasn't there—I was a lover calling back his long-gone woman, a jilted groom or a rebel, giving the finger to the establishment. I was whatever the song directed me to be.

That was why I didn't realize the engineer was tapping on the glass, waving his hands and desperately trying to get my attention. The music stopped, but I never used it as a guide—it was easier to sing from the heart. Until a hand was on my shoulder, I was soloing for a full minute. It was not recorded.

"What the feck?" I snapped. "This is the best take yet!"

Jerome shook his shaggy blond head apologetically.

"Sorry, man," the sound engineer sighed. "Your time is up. Axion P and his crew have the space."

Indignantly, I glowered at him.

It was a minute after eleven. One damn minute.

"Seriously?" I spat. "He couldn't wait ten minutes?"

"He booked the space," Jerome reminded me. "And you were running over time."

I was incensed. The rapper was never on time for anything, including his concerts. I highly doubted that Axion was there. Jerome was just covering his own ass in case the infamous hip-hop artist showed his face early. God forbid he had to wait.

"Sorry, man," Jerome said again, and I almost believed him.

You will be sorry, I thought, tossing the headphones from around my neck. One day soon, I'd be the one who made the studio staff jump for me. The following day, I had a meeting scheduled with Sony.

After almost a decade of working my tail to the bone, playing shitholes in Vegas and recording in garages, at last, I was getting a record deal.

I didn't bother to share this information with Jerome. That'd be right before he was informed we would no longer record with Muse Studios.

It'll be worth the look on his face. Even though I'd miss the place. It had its charms, and it had been a home away from my eclectic Santa Monica home.

"Whatever, man." Fearful of slipping the good news, I did not engage. I was known to unload data at inappropriate times.

I grabbed my electric guitar and packed it, careful not to catch my fingers in the heavy casing before locking it.

"You can leave that, man," Jerome said, sounding alarmed when he realized I was taking it with me. "You're back tomorrow, right?"

"Maybe."

I didn't bother to look at him, stalked toward the door, and moved down the halls of Muse, fuming.

There was no sign of Axion or his crew.

Such bullshit.

"You gonna punch something?" a voice chirped when I jabbed the down button for the elevator. I grimaced, seeing who it was.

You would know what I look like when I'm ready to clock something, The day was getting worse by the minute and it wasn't even noon. I should have looked both ways before leaving the sound booth. Miguel was always lurking around.

It's just one more reason to get the hell out of Muse. Good riddance to all you assholes.

"Probably," I conceded. "Are you offering your face?"

Miguel snickered and cast a sidelong look as he approached. Thankfully, I still made him uncomfortable.

"I caught your vocals earlier. You're sounding really good, Jayce. This album will be your best."

Sony thinks so.

"Thanks."

Damn, it was hard to be civil to that prick.

The stainless-steel doors opened and we stepped onto the lift. Miguel punched the lobby button as we stood in silence. It was strained, undoubtedly. Life was different in LA than the rest of the country. Things regarded as taboo to ordinary folk were commonplace behavior to Los Angelinos.

Things like your bandmates screwing your girlfriend.

Miguel, the bassist in my band, had been the first person I'd really bonded with in LA. Unfortunately for me, Teresa, my girlfriend of six months, had bonded with him too. Miguel had decided, "for the sake of the band," that he should seek other ventures after their fling had come to light, but I saw him in the studio more often than was agreeable.

There hadn't even been an apology; neither from Teresa nor Miguel, like I was overreacting and better grow thicker skin to make it in the cutthroat world I'd chosen.

Who knew? Maybe they were right. They had taught me a valuable lesson about trust and how not to have any.

As a result, I played nice with Miguel but couldn't help but distrust all the other bandmates too. Who else Teresa had been with? I mean, she'd sworn it was only once, and only with Miguel, but I didn't believe her, not when Miguel looked at me like he knew something I didn't.

Or maybe I was paranoid. LA had a way of making people loopy.

The doors slid open and I shoved past Miguel before he could move, a fleeting sense of satisfaction that I made it out first, but I realized how stupid it was to feel smug about something so petty.

If you're going to feel cocky about something, feel cocky about your meeting tomorrow. Nothing can destroy that feeling, It was a crisp morning. Thanksgiving was just around the corner and the air had a slight chill. Overhead, rain clouds slowly began to form over the valley in a depressing gray, and I idly wished I had a sweater. I grabbed my key fob and unlocked the 2014 Audi I'd bought a couple years back; my closest thing to a new car. I reminded myself I'd be getting a BMW any day ... as soon as that deal was signed.

Before backing out of my spot, I gazed at the studio—a steel structure with no warmth or personality. There had been three other studios before Muse and were bound to be dozens after.

Dozens. I am setting my sights high ...

Nothing wrong with that. I wouldn't be here if I didn't.

I peeled out of my spot like I intended to leave the place in the figurative dust, winding out of the city traffic toward my place near Palisades Park. At this hour of the morning there was not much transit but still, it was the city. My cell rang during this stop and go. I took it on my Bluetooth.

"Daryn," I laughed. "Talk to me."

"There he is!" my agent cooed through the speakers. "My rising star!"

That phrase made me cringe. I didn't particularly care for the reminder I hadn't fully risen.

"Are you guys ready for the meeting with Sony tomorrow?" Daryn asked, and I chuckled.

"Is anyone ever ready for something like that?" I replied. "Of course not."

"Good! Show them your sweet, humble side, Jayce. They love thinking they can mold you."

"You mean manipulate," I countered sardonically.

"Tsk, tsk, now don't be like that, Jayce. This is what we've been working toward. Your bandmates are anxious. You could stand to be a little more grateful."

If she could see the way my stomach was flipping, we wouldn't be having this conversation, but alas, all she saw was my cynical exterior.

"I am eternally grateful for all you've done," I told her sincerely. "Sony at 9:00."

"Oh no," she purred, her voice filling my ears from every section of the vehicle. "I have a surprise for you. Make sure you're there at 8:30."

"I don't like surprises." An image of Teresa popped into my head.

"I don't care."

I should have expected this from her. Daryn was not a woman to be argued with and I certainly would not fight her on something as trivial as a nice gesture.

"8:30 it is. Anything else?"

"Bring a nice pen. You'll want to remember the moment you signed the biggest deal of your life."

I chortled. "All right, Daryn."

"Toodles."

She disconnected the call, leaving me grinning. We really did owe Daryn a great deal. The success of our band, Rune, would have been limited to back-alley bars and opener shows without her.

She was a shark and well-known in the industry. Being on her roster was the next best thing to being coupled with Daniel Lanois.

And one day, maybe we'll be as big as U2.

She instinctively knew how to boost our image, what gigs to set up for us, our name. It was because of Daryn Jameson that I had gone from Jason Jensen to Jayce Joyce.

"I love the way it just rolls off the tongue," she'd said to me. "It's sexy, and sexy sells. No matter how talented you are, Jayce—and make no mistake, you are talented—it doesn't matter if your fans don't want to be bent over a table."

Sometimes I thought of bending Daryn over a table but suspected she'd own me if that situation ever arose. And I was most certainly not one to be on the bottom.

I steered the car into the carport and grabbed my guitar, locking the door before jogging up the front entrance. My bad mood completely diminished after speaking with Daryn even though fat drops of rain began to splatter against the pavement when I let myself in.

The sun was entirely blotted out and inside my small but awesome home, it was unusually dark for so early in the day.

I flipped on a few lights before plopping onto the couch, draping my legs atop the overstuffed cushions. My cell had six texts and I already knew without looking that they were from the band. The guys were deliriously happy about the future and who could blame them? We'd arrived where we'd aspired to be.

I stared at the phone for a long moment and got an overwhelming desire to call Mom. Ever since Sony had arranged for this meeting three weeks earlier, I'd wrestled with the same demon every time I was alone. I wanted to tell her the good news, but it wasn't to spread the joy—only so that she would tell my jerk father my "childish fantasy" would gross me more than he'd ever seen in his life.

Perhaps that wasn't true—I wasn't sure how much Sony was offering, but it had to be substantial.

It burned me that, after four years, I was still angry with my father, even though he'd acted as he always had, looking down on me like I wasn't worthy of the fame I'd worked so hard to reach.

I hadn't spoken to him since that Christmas and the relationship with my mom wasn't good either. When we did, she would force Micah on the phone but those conversations were short and awkward.

I tossed the cell aside before my fingers took over without my mind agreeing. Maybe I'd wait to give Mom an actual figure on our advance before making the call.

I was growing heavy-eyed. The rain always did that to me, creating a haze which made me want to nap.

At first I fought it, thinking about things to do today, but then I shoved the list aside and embraced the idea of a siesta. I'd earned it.

My lids barely closed before I was caught in a bizarre dream. I didn't remember a great deal but I saw my mom shaking her head at me. She kept repeating something before pointing over my shoulder. When I turned, Micah was staring at me with a blank expression on his face. He looked older and ... scared.

I pivoted back but my mother was gone and my dad was

standing there, his face covered in blood.

That was enough to spring me awake. At the same time, I realized it wasn't the only thing which had woken me—my cell was ringing too.

A full storm had taken hold while I napped, the wind picking up, the branches of the orange trees swinging wildly against the almost-black sky.

"Hello?" I mumbled, clearing my throat after the fact. If I'd looked at the call display, I would have seen it was a private number—not that it would have stopped me from answering it.

"Jason Jensen?"

I blinked several times, pulling the phone back to look at the caller. It told me nothing. It was weird to be called "Jason" after legally changing my name to Jayce Joyce many years ago. Nothing good would come from this call.

"Who is this?"

"Is this Jason Jenson?" the man sounded stern, authoritative, and my first thought was the IRS.

Outside, thunder rumbled and my jaw locked as I debated whether to tell him it was me.

"This is Detective Blake Corso of the Alpena Police Department. Is this Jason Jensen?"

A flash of lightning streaked the sky outside my living room window and I froze, knowing the horrific foreshadowing that only occurred in movies. My dream came flooding back to me full force and a sick feeling rocked my gut.

This wasn't a bad movie—it was my life, no matter how much of it seemed to play in slow motion.

"Yeah," I finally rasped. "This is he."

"Mr. Jensen, I'm afraid I have some bad news for you."

He didn't need to finish his thought. I already knew what he was going to say.

One of my parents had died.

CHAPTER TWO

Leila

Bad news always spreads through small towns like wildfire, and this instance was no different.

Sitting in Rosalie's Diner, having my morning coffee, all anyone could talk about was the horrible car accident from the night before and I wished they would stop. It gave me shivers every time I thought about it and it seemed that was all I could think about.

"He was drunk as a skunk," Sarah Millerson sighed, pouring from a pitcher as she shook her head. "Driving the wrong way on the freeway."

"It's a goddamn shame the driver in the semi survived," Pat Richards grunted. "That bastard should rot in hell."

"I'm sure he's in his own kind of hell this morning," Sarah replied softly, shooting me a look across the counter. "Imagine waking up and learning you killed someone. That's a hangover you'll never recover from."

"Killed someone?" Pat scoffed. "He did a lot more than that! He's a murdering son of a bitch. I hear his room at the hospital is under guard. Our tax dollars at work, huh? Protecting a piece of shit like that. I tell you, if he wasn't guarded, I'd go down there and get my own form of justice on that asshole, you know what I mean?"

I wanted to scream at him to stop it, my heart thudding madly as Pat grew more incensed. Sitting back, turning my eyes away from Pat's reddening face, I bit on my lower lip. Tears were burning behind my blue eyes but I willed myself not to cry.

I knew the Jensens, had even babysat Micah a few times over the years, which made the tragedy all the more real, but my heart was just as broken for the driver of that truck, drunk or not. I couldn't imagine what that man was going through.

It's easy for Pat to judge the man but I've seen him get behind the wheel after having a six-pack or more. It could just as easily have been Pat who made that fatal mistake.

Of course, these were not things I said aloud. I wasn't looking for a fight—not then and not ever. Leila Butler wasn't known for speaking her mind. I was more known for my quiet manner, a tender smile, and keeping the peace.

Except there was nothing peaceful about Rosalie's this morning, and the negativity was overwhelming.

"More coffee, hon?"

Sarah appeared before me, coffee jug in her weathered hands.

"No. Just the check, Sarah."

She nodded, casting me a final, worried gaze, and headed for the till. I grabbed my jacket from the neighboring stool and threw it over my shoulders.

"See ya, Leila!" Pat called after me, but I only waved at him without turning So he didn't see my expression. I wasn't much known for my poker face, something Sarah noticed when I stood by the register to pay.

"You shouldn't take these things to heart, hon," Sarah

mentioned softly when I handed her a ten-dollar bill. "There is nothing you can do about it."

"Doesn't make it any less heartbreaking," I muttered. "Keep the change."

She yelled out a thank-you but I was already out the door and halfway to my Jeep. I was pushing it for time, having spent too much of my morning eavesdropping on the regulars as they talked about the accident.

Accident. What a pathetic word for what happened. The whole thing could have been avoided with a little foresight.

I was far too distracted to drive and when I pulled up in the employee lot, I was glad I'd made it in one piece. I hoped the conversation at work wouldn't be the accident but the upcoming day didn't give me a good feeling. Turned out, I was right.

I quickly checked my reflection in the rearview mirror and ensured my honey-blonde hair was tucked under my hairnet. I wasn't wearing makeup, although I didn't need it. The freckles that had haunted me since childhood had diminished to a gentle dusting over my nose but I had been lucky enough to keep my youthful complexion. I looked tired, though, a slight darkness shadowing my usually bright eyes. It didn't matter—I had no one to impress at work.

No one to impress at home, either, I reminded myself dryly. Also not known for my social life.

Yeah, I wasn't known for a lot of things.

I pulled my keys from the ignition and started toward the side entrance. As I approached, at least fifty dayshift workers were milling about, chattering amongst themselves. Some had cigarettes dangling from between their lips while others were scowling, peering at Waxman Textiles, infuriated.

"What's going on?" I asked one of my coworkers. "Our shift starts in five minutes. Why is everyone out here?"

"We're locked out," Robin grunted.

"What?" It didn't make any sense. Most of us had worked here for years. If there was some kind of problem, we would have at least gotten an email ... wouldn't we?

On a whim, I pulled out my cell and checked my emails for an update but there nothing was nothing that indicated why we were standing around like fools.

I moved toward the door and pulled on it, feeling silly when it didn't give. Obviously, it had probably been done before.

"What a cowardly, shithead thing to do!" some guy yelled. I think his name was Thomas. He looked like a Tom.

"Don't jump to conclusions," I said, holding up my hand. I could feel tension brewing from a mile away and the last thing I wanted was to be in the middle of a riot, especially without all the facts.

"What else can it be?" Tom shot back. "They ain't giving us a paid vacation!"

Suddenly, the side door opened and, in a swarm, we marched toward Brad, the day manager, a rush of inquiries filling my ears.

"What's going on?"

"Are we working today or not?"

"Is there a setback?"

"What the hell is this?"

In a flash, Brad slapped a piece of paper on the door and ducked back inside.

A weird silence followed his departure and I was left dumbly staring at Robin.

"What does it say?" someone yelled and again, we all swept forward in a wave, craning our necks to read the notice Brad had pasted to the door.

"You have got to be shitting me!" Tom howled. "They're laying us off! Just like that! No notice, nothing!"

An uproar began and I wanted to get out of there before shit started flying.

I backed out from the angry mob of workers, retreated to my car, and observed from there. My heart was hammering in my chest as the gravity of what had happened struck me.

I was unemployed. One minute, I'd had a comfortable job, a guaranteed paycheck and insurance benefits; the next, I was locked out and left for broke without so much as a handshake and "good luck."

Look at them, I thought grimly, watching as the workers began to pound on the entrance. *What good will this do?*

I couldn't sit around gaping at my workplace all day, but it was like a train wreck and I couldn't look away until my cell rang several minutes later.

"Hon, did you just get locked out of Waxman?" my mother crooned in my voice. She sounded as stressed out as I felt.

"Yeah ... how did you hear about it so fast?"

She sighed heavily. "It's a small town, Leila. Jake Watts called. He's livid. He has four kids to support!"

I closed my eyes and shook my head. We weren't unionized. There was nothing we could do unless we hired a lawyer to clap back and Waxman must have known we had no means to do that.

How can we, when the pay was minimal?

"This day is a write-off," I asserted, and Mom soundly commiserated.

"Come over, sweetie. I'll bake a pie."

I laughed. Her solution to everything was baking or cooking. My mom was a quintessential housewife. That classification was derogatory in our ever-changing society but she'd have said the same thing.

Nothing made her happier than caring for her husband and kids, even though we were all grown and living on our own.

She'd married my dad just out of high school and spent her life caring for the four of us, working not a single day. What was peculiar in today's world came naturally to Mom, like she was from another era. It didn't bother her in the least that other women had full-time careers. In her mind, being at home with her family was the right thing to do.

All she needs is a gaggle of grandkids to spoil and she'll be content.

My sister Cat was a newlywed and my brother, Ryan, had recently married as well. I knew kids were in the near future.

I ignored the stab of envy and refocused on what Mom had suggested. I considered her offer. My day was freed up, after all. What else could I do but go home and stress about being unemployed?

And she baked a delectable pie.

"All right, Mom, I'll be there in fifteen."

Outside, a real riot was breaking out and my jaw clenched as I watched my colleagues hurling random items at the building. A part of me wanted to stop them but the meek side of me won, as always. Conflict was not my thing and conflict resolution was hardly my specialty. What could I possibly say to a bunch of desperate people to make them stand down, anyway?

"Hey, morons, they've got the property damage you're causing on camera!"

"Tom, you can't break into the building with a cinderblock!"

It was better to just opt out of here. I backed out of my space and left the lot, my eyes darting worriedly to the rearview mirror. Security joined the assembly. Thankfully, I was the hell out of there. A criminal record was not on my list of wants; my prospects were bleak enough as it was.

It took me less than fifteen minutes to get to my parents' place. Only after I parked in front of the perfectly manicured lawn did it dawn on me that I had defied all the speed limits, putting as much space between me and the factory as possible.

My heart was still beating fast as I made my way up the flagstone. A light snow had fallen overnight and it dusted the Thanksgiving decorations Mom had put out. A plywood turkey eyed a cornucopia filled with squash and a huge real pumpkin sat on the front porch.

Mom put a lot of effort into her décor but it was hard to feel festive today, not when a cloud of gloom seemed to have befallen Alpena.

I should have stayed in bed this morning, Wrapping the jacket around me, I stepped onto the wraparound veranda. I blamed my lethargy on the cold but maybe I'd sensed the bleakness of the day instinctively.

Too late now—I was facing whatever was in store for me.

Mom must have been watching from the window because the door flew open the second my foot hit the landing. She peered at me with worried blue eyes.

"Oh honey," she said sympathetically, extending her arms to me. "Come here."

Instantly, I threw myself into her arms, relishing the warmth of her bosom. My feelings shone clearly on my face, no matter how hard I tried to hide them.

"It's fine." I didn't separate myself from her embrace. "I'll find another job."

"Of course you will!" Carla Butler conceded firmly. "You have many talents!"

Sometimes I wondered how she managed to lie with such a serious face. The fact was I didn't have many talents. I'd graduated high school, but much to my dad's chagrin, I'd never attended college.

"You're the only one who did not go to college!" he protested. "Why not?"

"Because I don't know what to do with my life and will not waste your money on a degree I might never use."

"Leila, a college education is important! At least a trade school like Morris!"

"I'm not going to be a mechanic like my brother, Dad."

No, I thought with sarcasm, pissed for not listening to my father five years ago. *Instead I'll work a menial job and get laid off on a whim. That is a much sounder plan.*

Waxman had been the first and only job I'd ever had. It had been supposed to be something to guide me to where I wanted to go, but what direction was that? Even still, I had no idea.

"Come on, sweetie. Help me cut the apples."

We untangled from one another and I followed my mom into the kitchen.

"Whoa! Are you opening a pie shop?" I asked, noting the pile of apples on the kitchen island. "

"I'm making a few pies," she replied defensively. "I'm taking them to the neighbors and …"

To my astonishment, she bit her lower lip, blinking back some tears. It was not difficult to surmise where my heart-on-the-sleeve responses were from. Mom could cry at the drop of a hat. She could full-on sob at cat-food commercials.

"Mom! What's wrong?" I demanded, rushing to her side. "Why are you crying?"

"Oh," she uttered, waving her hand and blinking rapidly. "It's just so sad. I, I'm making some pies for the Jensens."

My back tensed and I parked on a stool at the counter, nodding slowly.

"I see …"

Because the entire topic was too painful, I did not insist, but had to know and if anyone had an answer, it was Mom.

"What is happening over there?"

She looked at me in shock, her eyes widening. "You didn't hear about what happened?"

"I did," I replied quickly. "I only meant ... what's happening with Micah now?"

My mom took her own seat, peering at me from across the counter, her mouth pulled into a fine line of regret.

"Well, I imagine he'll go to Children's Services," she sighed. "That's what happens when you lose both your parents ..."

She choked on the last words, making me shudder. I swallowed and shook my head, the now-familiar sorrow filling my heart. Micah was an orphan; his parents dead from a misfortune.

How much worse could it be for a kid of ten?

The only thing worse was the estranged older brother re-entering Micah's life.

Jayce Joyce is too self-centered to return to Alpena. Micah is better off without him ... isn't he?

CHAPTER THREE

Jayce

Most of the people at the house were strangers to me, and they certainly didn't know me, but that didn't stop the dirty looks I was getting.

My parents' neighbors and friends filtered through the house, mumbling empty platitudes into my ears, but I didn't hear it. I was still in shock, stunned this had taken place.

"It was a drunken truck driver who hit them, Mr. Jensen. He was on the wrong side of the interstate as your father was driving. He tried to swerve but ... death was instant ... fortunately, Micah was at a sleepover ... make arrangements ..."

What the cop said still flittered in and out of my subconscious. Most of it was baffling, partly because I wasn't there in mind at all. My thoughts wondered why I hadn't made amends with Dad when I'd had the chance to make things right. Why had he always been so damned stubborn?

I didn't even bother to answer the door when someone rang the bell any longer. The kid who I assumed was my brother did that, although I wouldn't have recognized him on the street if I'd seen him. Micah looked nothing like the six-year-old I'd left behind almost four years ago. However, he looked like the young man from my dream.

The premonition stayed, hovering over me like an umbrella, and every time I closed my eyes, trying to block the outside world, it would flood back in a torrent.

The kitchen my mom had loved so much was overflowing with casseroles and roasts, pies and breads. It appeared like a buffet had vomited inside; the smells of the food made me nauseous. I wished people would stop coming in, but in a town the size of Alpena, peace wasn't something easily found. They meant well, but I wished they do it somewhere else.

"Just lock the damned door!" I finally snapped at Micah, my nerves stretched to their breaking point. "No more people!"

He looked at me with blank eyes and the expression slightly chilled me. There was no emotion in his face, nor any sadness or depression. It was like he was elsewhere and his body moved around on autopilot.

"YOU lock the damned door," he snapped back. Even though I'd started it, his attitude jolted me.

Without a word of rebuke, I rose from the chair and approached the front door, hoping to close it before another person came by offering condolences, but of course, I wasn't so lucky.

Two women were coming up to the porch, and for a twisted second, I wanted to slam the door in their faces until it flashed upon me that I actually knew them. Well, I recognized *her* anyway.

I couldn't remember the last time I'd seen Leila Butler, but certainly, whenever it was, she had not looked like *this*.

A vague recollection of a freckled-face blonde with wide, pensive eyes and slightly bucked teeth was in my mind.

Chapter Three

Braces and corrective surgery had done miracles on the lithe, tall woman in a simple white T-shirt under a long cardigan and pair of form-fitting jeans that left nothing to the imagination. Despite the inappropriateness of the situation, as she neared the door with her mother, I found myself gawking at her.

Carla Butler was holding a stack of pies in her hands and froze when her eyes rested on me.

"Jason!" she gasped. "Y-you're here!"

My brow furrowed at the absurdity of the disclosure.

"Of course I'm here. Where else would I be?"

The Butler women exchanged glances and Carla looked at me again but Leila shifted her eyes away. I got the sense she was still checking me out peripherally, but it was tough to discern. Maybe it was just wishful thinking not to feel like such a pervert for gawking at her.

"I, I'm sorry for your loss, Jason," Carla said, holding out the pies. "I admired your mother a lot. And your father."

She added Dad as an afterthought. He really had been a prick.

And now he was dead.

"Thanks," I grunted, accepting the desserts. I didn't know how much the neighbors supposed we could consume, but most of it would certainly go to waste.

"H-how are you holding up?" she asked. Yet another stupid question, but I kept studying Leila's profile.

"Fine." I wished Leila looked at me but she was distracted by something else.

"Hi, Micah," she called.

My brother joined me in the entrance. "Hi, Leila!"

There was genuine emotion in his voice and his eyes brightened up.

Oh, look at that—he is in there.

Micah pushed past me and stepped onto the porch, looking up at Leila with shining eyes.

"I'm so sorry about your mom and dad," she sighed softly, stooping down to meet him at eye level. "Is there anything you need? Anything I can do for you?"

As if I wasn't even there! I was beginning to take it slightly personally. After all, I'd lost my parents too. Where was her compassion for me? I hadn't been asked if I needed something.

Or was I being egotistical?

To my annoyance, Micah turned and looked at me, his dark eyes narrowing. Leila also peered at me for the first time with contempt.

What the hell is this? Why is she looking at me like that? I haven't seen her since she was a teen! Anything she heard about me is secondhand. What a judgmental bitch!

Deliberately, Micah turned to her again and shook his head, but the message was clear—he didn't want me there.

"No," he assured. "I'm fine."

Leila straightened up and intentionally avoided eye contact but I could tell she wanted to stare me down. As if I was somehow responsible for everything that had happened.

Have I walked into an ambush?

I recognized the sense of ire growing in my stomach. I felt it every time I returned to Alpena.

Here I am, back again, and facing everyone's scrutiny.

"Do you have a cell?" Leila asked my brother, but her voice was low as if she'd suddenly realized her mom and I had too much interest in the exchange. A red tinge touched her face.

"Of course."

"Get it and I'll program my number in it. Call me anytime you need anything."

I had never seen anyone move as fast as Micah in that

instant, leaving me and the Butler women awkwardly gaping at one another.

Carla nervously cleared her throat and shot her daughter an odd look.

"And ... Jason, of course you can call us too," Carla offered lamely, but decidedly, the sentiment did not extend to me.

"Sure," I grunted. "Thanks."

"Have you made arrangements for the ... services?" Carla asked timidly. "We would like to pay our respects."

I nodded. "Friday at four is the funeral. There's a viewing on Thursday from 3-7 p.m. at Chapel Rock."

"We'll be there," Carla assured me. Oddly, I took comfort in knowing that, even though I sensed the near animus oozing from her. It was good to know there would be two familiar faces in the sea of angst and brimstone.

"Great." It was not easy to be grateful when their thoughts were clear—they didn't think I belonged there.

I don't want to be here either! I'm supposed to be in LA, meeting with Sony right now, not accepting desserts and empty sentiments from strangers.

Shit! Sony.

As impossible as it seemed, I'd forgotten about the meeting. My cell had been off since I'd boarded the plane in LA, and I had not bothered to turn it on again when I got to Michigan.

"Excuse me." Micah came running back to the door, but I brushed past him.

He didn't need me—he'd made that much clear from the minute I arrived. He had more friends than me in Alpena.

The flight had been a blur; the cab ride to the house and the conversations with the people did not register in my mind yet. Not a single person cared enough about me, but slowly, the haze was lifting from my eyes and I located my cell in the pocket of my jacket. I needed to touch base with Daryn, at the very least. The rest of the band could wait.

When I turned on the phone, it exploded with texts and voicemail notifications. I barely managed to open my contacts when it rang again. It was Daryn. She probably had been trying incessantly to get through.

"Hey." It was the only word I could muster. She didn't give me time to create a sentence.

"Hey? Fucking HEY? Is that what you're saying to me? Do you realize how much you dropped the ball? I sent a limo to your house at 8:30 this morning. A fucking Hummer, Jayce, fully stocked with a—"

"My parents died last night."

At least I knew what her surprise was. Too bad I couldn't muster the least bit of excitement.

The silence which followed could've been cut with a knife. I fell back on the bed in the guestroom, blankly staring at the ceiling. Out of the blue, the reality hit me like a thousand tons of mass.

"What?" Daryn finally managed to say. "Jayce, are you serious?"

I inhaled deeply but couldn't breathe, not really. My chest hurt and I was almost in tears.

Goddamn it!

I gritted my teeth together, trying to catch my breath.

"Jayce, are you there?"

"Yeah." The word barely managed to get out.

"What happened? Where are you?"

"I'm in Michigan. The funeral's in a couple days."

"Christ, I am so sorry, Jayce. Obviously if I'd known, I wouldn't have gone off on you. Why didn't you call me?"

The answers couldn't formulate—my mind wasn't working that way yet.

"Can you do me a favor?"

"Anything! Do you want me to come down there? Do you need me to make arrangements? Tell me!"

"NO!" The last thing I wanted was for her to come. The next few days were inconceivable, and Daryn shouldn't see me in pieces. In her presence, things were purely professional, and there was no cause for her to see me unstable, no matter the circumstances.

"No," I said again, with less emotion. "Just tell the guys what's up. Did you go to the meeting today?"

"Never mind the meeting."

The answer filled me with dismay. It was enough—I'd screwed the opportunity; the one we'd been busting our asses for. The guys would never forgive me.

"Will you do that?" I was floating again, somewhere else, somewhere by the ceiling. I barely recognized myself, lying there on the bed. There was no semblance of the brooding rock-star. Suddenly I was a little boy who'd lost his parents, making sense of everything that was happening.

"Of course I will," Daryn sighed. "Are you sure you don't want me to come out there?"

"I'm sure."

"Okay, Jayce ...if there's anything you need, anything at all ..."

"I'll be in touch. My phone may be off sometimes."

"I won't bother you. Call anytime."

I nodded even though I knew she couldn't see me and disconnected the call without saying goodbye.

Remaining in my spot, looking at the white swirls on the ceiling, trying to make sense of the lot. The more I thought, the less coherent my life seemed.

A knock on the door shifted my attention and even though I didn't answer, it opened anyway.

Carla Butler stood at the threshold, looking uncomfortable.

"Jason ..."

I turned my head toward her without sitting up. I thought about telling her my name was Jayce, but it wasn't worth the energy. She didn't care what my name was anyway.

"Leila and I are going to stay for a while, if you don't mind. Micah has asked us."

My body heaved into a vertical position.

"No need for that. We've got this."

"Well ... you have a visitor," Carla announced.

"So? People have been coming in and out all day."

"No, Jason, this is someone different."

Why was she being so enigmatic and not saying what she wanted to say?

"Mrs. Butler, with all due respect, my headspace is not ready to play twenty questions."

"It's your parents' lawyer."

What!? Not that I had experience in these matters before, but it seemed an odd time to be discussing the estate, didn't it? My parents weren't even out of the morgue yet.

"Now?"

Carla looked at me awkwardly and lowered her eyes.

"This needs to be dealt with sooner rather than later, Jason."

Again, I wished she'd speak in layman's terms for my overwrought mind. She seemed to sense my chagrin but when she spoke again, the world turned that much darker.

"Custody of Micah, Jason. Your parents named you his guardian in the event of something like this."

If you want to continue reading this story, you can get your copy from your favorite vendor by searching for the title:

Home is Where the Heat Is

A Secret Baby Christmas Romance

You can also find the e-book version by typing this link in your computer's browser:

https://www.hotandsteamyromance.com/products/home-is-where-the-heat-is-a-secret-baby-christmas-romance

OTHER BOOKS BY THIS AUTHOR

Saving Her Rescuer: A Billionaire & A Virgin Romance

I was just trying to get away from my crazy ex for the weekend when I ended up in a giant pileup on the highway up to Gore Mountain.

https://geni.us/SavingHerRescuer

Sensual Sounds: A Rockstar Ménage

Lust. Lies. Double lives.

The rock and roll industry is full of people who are looking out for themselves and willing to do anything to rise to the top.

https://www.hotandsteamyromance.com/collections/frontpage/products/sensual-sounds-a-rockstar-menage

On the Run: A Secret Baby Romance

Murder. Lies. Fraud. Just another day in the lives of billionaires and women on the run.

https://www.hotandsteamyromance.com/collections/frontpage/products/on-the-run-a-secret-baby-romance

The Dirty Doctor's Touch: A Billionaire Doctor Romance

I am a master. An elitist. I am at the top of my field, and I know what I am doing.

https://www.hotandsteamyromance.com/collections/frontpage/products/the-dirty-doctor-s-touch-a-billionaire-doctor-romance

∽

The Hero She Needs: A Single Daddy Next Door Romance

He's the only man I've ever wanted...

https://www.hotandsteamyromance.com/collections/frontpage/products/the-hero-she-needs-a-single-daddy-next-door-romance

∽

You can find all of my books here

Hot and Steamy Romance
https://www.hotandsteamyromance.com

ABOUT THE AUTHOR

Mrs. Love writes about smart, sexy women and the hot alpha billionaires who love them. She has found her own happily ever after with her dream husband and adorable 6 and 2 year old kids.
Currently, Michelle is hard at work on the next book in the series, and trying to stay off the Internet.
"Thank you for supporting an indie author. Anything you can do, whether it be writing a review, or even simply telling a fellow reader that you enjoyed this. Thanks

facebook.com/HotAndSteamyRomance
instagram.com/michellesromance

©Copyright 2020 by Scarlett King & Michelle Love - All rights Reserved
In no way is it legal to reproduce, duplicate, or transmit any part of this document in either electronic means or in printed format. Recording of this publication is strictly prohibited and any storage of this document is not allowed unless with written permission from the publisher. All rights are reserved.
Respective authors own all copyrights not held by the publisher.

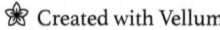 Created with Vellum

www.ingramcontent.com/pod-product-compliance
Lightning Source LLC
LaVergne TN
LVHW011725060526
838200LV00051B/3033